Perfect.

It fit into his hand. His fingers bent and gripped the leather. Leather, these balls were real leather. He started to dribble without thinking, and everything started to feel better. The sound of the ball bouncing. The rhythm and the bounce. Against the floor and into his hands. Between his legs, back and forth. Behind the back. Dribble. Head up. Ball low.

Other books by
NORA RALEIGH BASKIN

In the Company of Crazies

BaskeTBaLL
(OR soMethinG Like iT)

NORA RALEIGH BASKIN

🔲 HarperTrophy®
An Imprint of HarperCollins Publishers

Basketball (or Something Like It)
Copyright © 2005 by Nora Raleigh Baskin
All rights reserved. Printed in the United States of America. No part
of this book may be used or reproduced in any manner whatsoever
without written permission except in the case of brief quotations
embodied in critical articles and reviews. For information address
HarperCollins Children's Books, a division of HarperCollins
Publishers, 1350 Avenue of the Americas, New York, NY 10019.
www.harpercollinschildrens.com

Library of Congress Cataloging-in-Publication Data
Baskin, Nora Raleigh.
    Basketball (or something like it) / Nora Raleigh Baskin.—1st ed.
        p.   cm.
    Summary: Hank, Nathan, Jeremy, and Anabel deal with the
realities of middle school basketball, including family pressure, a
series of coaches with very different personalities and agendas,
and what it means to be a team—and a friend.
    ISBN-10: 0-06-059612-0
    ISBN-13: 978-0-06-059612-5
    [1. Basketball—Fiction.   2. Sportsmanship—Fiction.
3. Interpersonal relations—Fiction.   4. Self-realization—Fiction.
5. Family life—Connecticut—Fiction.   6. Connecticut—Fiction.]
I. Title.
PZ7.B29233Bas 2005   2004005743
[Fic]—dc22

Typography by Amy Ryan
❖
First Harper Trophy edition, 2007

For my boys, with all my love:
Sam, who inspired this story and
continues to inspire me every day.
Ben, who read every word—commented, corrected,
but mostly supported me as he always has.
And Steve, my husband, who came home
with an idea, then challenged me to write it.

And once again to my invaluable young readers,
Erin and Brigit Anderson (and their mom),
Daniel and Greg Berger (and their mom, too),
Alexander Pachman, and Hank Kaufman.
Thank you.

And to my editor, Maria Modugno, and my agent,
Nancy Gallt. Thank you both. So much.

THE NORTH BRIDGE FORUM

NORTH BRIDGE BASKETBALL TEAM MAKES IT TO SEMIFINALS

THE NORTH BRIDGE PANTHERS have surprised all the basketball pundits by making it to the semifinals of the state high school tournament in the Class S division. State top seed Colby High and the sixteenth-seeded Panthers battled it out in a classic game on Monday night. Even though the Panthers were the decided underdogs in the quarterfinals, the players felt confident that they would prevail. North Bridge narrowly defeated Colby High 67–65 on Monday evening in a game played in the Roton, Connecticut, field house.

"Games are won or lost at the foul line," winning coach Pat Trimboli stated after the victory. "Tonight we made our shots, and we'll just have to see what happens Friday night. The kids are confident."

According to Trimboli, scouts from the University of Connecticut and even Virginia and Tennessee will be coming to the semifinal game. It's no secret which one of the Panthers they are going to be watching.

The winner of tonight's semifinals will play for the state crown next Tuesday. If North Bridge wins, then they will play for their first ever state championship. However, according to the team captain, these kids have been working toward this moment since long before they ever got to high school.

(con't. on page B6)

SIXTH
GRADE

THE CLINICS

Hank

Hank heard everything while he was brushing his teeth, getting ready for bed. His parents were downstairs talking about him, again. And basketball. Again.

"Don't think they don't do it on purpose," Hank's dad was saying.

Clanking and clinking.

"That's ridiculous." His mother's reply.

Hank could hear their voices moving around the kitchen and into the living room and back. His mother was cleaning up from dinner, which explained the clanking and clinking.

"Why else would they schedule this basketball clinic at the same time as soccer? And don't think they didn't *know* about the soccer playoffs. Because they do."

Turning the tap water on didn't drown out their voices. Hank stared at himself in the mirror, his mouth foamy with toothpaste.

"So call somebody and complain. . . ." This was his mother's brilliant suggestion.

"Somebody! Like who? Like Joel Bischoff? If Hank misses all the clinics and screws up at the tryout, who do you think is going to look better?"

"Who?"

"Who? Are you kidding? His own son, that's who."

Upstairs, Hank spit toothpaste into the sink. It couldn't have been better timing. He felt like spitting. He imagined his parents could see him, only it wasn't the sink, it was the floor. Right in front of their faces. He imagined they would stop, stop talking about *him* all the time. Stop talking about basketball or baseball or whatever season and whatever sport they felt Hank should be getting more playing time in playing a better position.

"You mean Tyler Bischoff?" Hank's mother asked, and answered her own question. "Hank is five times better than Tyler Bischoff. Ten times."

His father was silent. Hank figured he was making *that* face. That face that says, "Isn't it obvious?"

As in, isn't it obvious that Joel Bischoff would

want Hank Adler to miss all the pre-tryout clinics and screw up completely and be cut from the travel basketball team so that his kid would have a better chance? And that that is obviously why he scheduled the clinics for Wednesday nights. Soccer night.

Hank's parents had the conspiracy theory down to an art.

"Well, somebody should say something," Hank's mother said again, but a little more quietly. Then he heard his mother's determined footsteps leave the room.

Oh God, Hank thought. He felt a headache coming on. No, he definitely had a headache already. He knew just what his mother was going to do. And Hank knew, even if his mother didn't, that that was exactly what his father wanted. She was going to call "somebody." Probably not Tyler Bischoff's dad, who was on the basketball board, but somebody. Somebody's mom maybe, and get them all worked up. Maybe two or three other select moms from the soccer team. And then she'd go in for the kill.

He wasn't sure how it worked exactly, because she did all her heavy phone calling during school hours. She even had one of those headsets that strapped around her head and plugged into her ear, like she worked for the Secret Service.

Only one thing was for certain; Hank knew she'd

make a big stink, and they either would or would not change the dates for the clinic, or change the time of the soccer playoffs for the entire county. New flyers would go out, or more angry phone calls would ensue, and some people would think it was great while just as many would get pissed as hell. But most surely, Hank would be going to every one of those basketball clinics.

And he'd have to wonder the whole time if his parents had totally ruined his chance of making the basketball team at all.

Nathan

Nathan knew better than to ask his dad. He had said no last season, and Nathan had spent the whole year having to hear from the travel basketball kids at school about all the games and other towns, the fights with the referees, the fights with kids on the other teams, the fights with the *parents* of kids on the other teams. And everybody always asking Nathan why he wasn't playing.

They just assumed. They just asked him why he wasn't playing, as if *had* he tried out, of course, he would have made the team. Of course, because he was black. Nathan was the only black kid in the whole North Bridge sixth grade. No, that wasn't exactly true. There had been one other. A girl. But she and her family moved to North Carolina in the middle of October.

So how come you're not on the team, Nathan?

They just assumed.

Nathan felt the same way except that he knew the answer. His father wouldn't let him. So this year he decided not to ask.

Nathan stared at the ceiling. He needed a plan. He rolled over and faced his clock radio. It was 11:34. He readjusted his blanket. He even sat up and tried to touch his toes, which poked up like two woolen, miniature mountains. He lay back down with a thud. It was 11:35.

No plan yet.

Jeremy

" I think you should do this, Jeremy," his grandmother said. She was going through Jeremy's backpack. It had been a long time since she had done anything like this. In fact, when her kids were little she *never* did anything like this. She didn't remember all these papers coming home from school. And all the different colors. All these announcements.

But now she was taking the time. She read them all. She wanted to make sure she didn't miss anything. This time she would do it right.

"I don't want to do anything," Jeremy answered. He was sitting at the kitchen table eating a snack. He needed a haircut, his grandmother thought, but she didn't say anything. It might have been a long time since she had little kids to take care of, but some things never change. One thing at a time, she thought. I'll start with this first. I'll mention the hair later tonight.

"It's basketball, Jeremy," she said. She was certain she remembered Jeremy playing basketball when he lived with his father in Central City. In a big building right in the middle of the city, some kind of center. A church-sponsored center with two big doors and nowhere to park her car. It was run-down, she remembered. The bathroom was down these long stairs, and there was rude graffiti all over the walls inside the stall. It must have been summer, because it was brutally hot inside the gym, but Jeremy played there. And he was good. She thought she remembered that, too. Yes, he was good.

"I don't care," Jeremy answered. "I'm fine, Grandma."

He always said that: "I don't care." When she asked him about school he always had the same answer for that, too. "Fine." She didn't push. His father's girlfriend had dropped him off only two months ago. Two days before school here in North Bridge started.

"I can't take care of him anymore," Lannie had said. Jeremy was standing right next to her when she said it. She never even came inside.

"What do you mean, Lannie? Where's his father? Where's Ron?" Jeremy's grandmother asked, although, looking back, she wished she hadn't said anything. Every night she rolled over restlessly in her bed. She wished she could go back and do it all over again. She wished she had just smiled and said, "Oh that's wonderful. Now Jeremy can live with me! I'm so happy."

Because she *was* happy. It was so wonderful to have her son's only son living in her house. He looked so much like his father. It was so wonderful to have a second chance.

"I don't know. I just know I can't take care of Jeremy no more," Lannie said it again. And then she left. No word from Jeremy's father. Nothing else. And now Jeremy was here.

It was wonderful and it was so hard.

"I remember you were really good. You made lots of points," his grandmother tried again. "I'll tell you what. You don't have to join the team, but why don't you go to these three basketball clinics and just see how you like it. You might like it."

"No thanks," Jeremy said. He was always polite. He had finished his apples and peanut butter, and his grandmother knew she was going to lose her opportunity.

"I'll pay you," she blurted out.

Jeremy looked up.

Jeremy

But the next morning Jeremy was sure he didn't want to play basketball.

He didn't know why. Even if it had been about the commitment, Jeremy wouldn't know it. He didn't have the words, but sometimes his skin felt too tight on his body. It was almost as if he couldn't bear the feeling one more second. Sometimes he'd notice that his fists were balled up for no reason. When he shook out his fingers, his hand hurt. He'd wake up in the morning and his jaw would ache from clenching his teeth all night.

"Are you awake, Jeremy?" his grandmother was calling from downstairs. She worked at the post office, and she had to leave before the middle-school bus came.

Her voice sent the memory of whatever Jeremy

had been dreaming about right out of his head. He lay under the covers for a while. Nothing was familiar yet. Not the ceiling, the light, the window. The smell of this room. Nothing felt right.

"Time to get up," his grandmother tried again.

Just a couple of months ago, back home, Lannie wouldn't have bothered calling for him. She would have still been sleeping when Jeremy had to get up for school. The noise from the street would have wakened him. Or a siren outside. Or a dog barking. Or someone in the apartment above slamming a door. Usually Jeremy just woke up on his own, startled by the hope that his father had come home sometime during the night.

But of course, he hadn't.

Now Jeremy could hear his grandmother coming up the stairs, slowly. She was kind of old, and it was probably hard for her. Old people are always saying they hate stairs.

Just as she got to the door, Jeremy called out, "I'm up. I'm getting up."

She must hate having to do this all over again. Have some dumb kid in her house, even if it was her only grandchild. She didn't want him here in the first place. You could just tell by the way she had asked Lannie where Jeremy's father was. That was the first thing out of her mouth.

"Okay." His grandmother's voice moved back down the stairs. "I'll be home early. Your lunch is on the counter."

Jeremy waited until he heard her footsteps start down the stairs again.

He shouted, "Thanks!" She wasn't really so bad. She was trying pretty hard. She was a real good cook. She made really good sandwiches. But still Jeremy knew he couldn't stay.

Not here.

Jeremy wondered if she would be upset when he left. Probably; grandmothers are like that. And now, well, he'd have to stay at least until after those stupid basketball clinics because he had promised. Jeremy looked over at the brand-new clock radio his grandmother had just bought for him and felt guilty. He hadn't just promised. He had gotten paid to promise.

Maybe he'd even stay and try out for the basketball team, but then, after that, he'd leave.

He'd have to do it soon. Before they got too used to each other.

Anabel

Maybe it was her name, Anabel. What an awful name. A perfect name to ensure that you are never taken seriously, although Anabel doubted it would have made much of a difference. What made a difference, at least to her father, was Michael. Michael playing basketball and being good at basketball, and Anabel hated basketball.

It wasn't exactly the game she hated, or even the ball or the dusty, echoey gyms she had been dragged to since her earliest memory. Actually, basketball was fun if you took out the parents, the arguments, the tension, the expectations. No, it wasn't basketball she hated. It was the importance of it.

The sheer magnitude.

Basketball came before everything. If her brother had a practice, or camp, or a clinic, or (God forbid) a *Game*, everything else could (and would) wait. Except eating, since you had to eat to play well. And shopping, as long as you were shopping for the right sneakers, compression shorts, or quick-drying sports socks.

For Michael.

Maybe it had gotten worse when their mother stopped coming to the games, but surely it had started long before then. Anabel could remember her father screaming from the bleachers at basketball games as early as second grade, and before basketball became Michael's sole focus, it had been soccer. Before that it was baseball. But first it had been T-ball.

Back then, they both played. Michael and Anabel. Except when Michael turned six (Anabel was still five), T-ball became unacceptable. Unacceptable for Michael. Their dad called the league president.

"I've been pitching to my son from the mound since he was three years old, for Christ's sake," Mr. Morrisey insisted. "So for Michael T-ball would just be a complete waste of time."

Wasting time was a dreadful sin. Missed chances. Precious skill-building opportunities were not to be taken lightly. *Opportunity* being the operative word here.

In reality, Michael was only eleven months older than Anabel. But they ended up in the same grade, Anabel being one of the youngest and Michael the oldest. Being the oldest didn't hurt when it came to athletics, but it did mean Michael missed the August fifteenth cutoff date to turn seven and play official Little League.

The president of the North Bridge Baseball Association wouldn't budge, and Michael was condemned to another year of organized T-ball. Only shortly thereafter, Michael Morrisey and his photocopied, semilegible birth certificate turned up at Little League sign-ups in the next town over.

"Yes, of course he's seven years old," Mr. Morrisey told the guys at the sign-up table. He said it with a clear-conscience, straight face that Anabel would never forget.

Of course, Anabel couldn't play T-ball in North Bridge anymore, although it wasn't ever entirely clear why. Was it because the logistics of getting Anabel and Michael to two different games in two different towns would be too hard? Or was it simply because Mr. Morrisey was blacklisted for that entire year in North Bridge?

So instead Anabel sat in the grass and played with her Legos while her brother stood terrified with the bat on his shoulder for three months. Anabel remembered her mother bringing sandwiches and drinks in a red-and-white cooler. She liked baseball because it was outside. She loved picnicking with her mother and playing at the schools that had playgrounds by the baseball field.

She will always remember that summer as the last summer her mother had nothing better to do than lay in the sun and braid Anabel's hair. It was the summer before her mother started working. Anabel and her mother watched the clouds glide smoothly across the darkening sky, sprayed bug spray all over their bodies, and cheered on Michael's team.

Looking back, Anabel was sure she had been just as happy, just as content, even *relieved* that it was her brother rounding second, getting thrown out at third, with two outs, down by one, in the bottom of the sixth inning. Even when her brother was winning, kicking the winning goal, or shooting a basket to tie the score, Anabel was relieved it wasn't her.

It was easier to sit in the grass, munching on pretzels, than to risk finding out you're no good.

Anabel

Things started really going downhill the year Michael won the fourth-grade hotshot contest at the Hoops for Heart fund-raiser. Mr. Morrisey felt he had found his son's real athletic niche. That was two years, hundreds of spectator hours, countless concession stand lunches (sometimes dinners), and several demanding phone calls later. It was also the year Anabel and Michael's mother got her big promotion and started traveling for work.

Anabel's mother said she had thought about it for months. Should she? Or shouldn't she? It would mean she'd be away from the family a lot. But it was a lot more money. And it was a great opportunity.

(There was that word—*opportunity*—again.)

After their mother took the position, Anabel and Michael's father never talked about it again. Whether it had been a good idea or not. Whether it was working out for everyone or not. It didn't matter.

The tunnel he had begun digging, through which Michael would dribble, pass, and shoot, was now big enough to bury them all inside. Basketball was everything, and somehow Anabel got relegated to the sidelines. Her territory was reading directions to the games and then reversing them to get home. Sometimes running out to the car for an extra bottle of Gatorade. At halftime or before a game, when she had finished her homework or her one hundredth paperback book, Anabel might dribble around and shoot a little. And wait to go home.

Basketball was everything.

And it was all done in the name of Michael.

What Anabel's father did not seem to notice was, because she was spending so much time in gyms and basketball courts, his daughter could pretty consistently go ten for ten from the free throw line and had a solid 40 percent three-point average.

In fact, Anabel herself barely noticed.

Nathan

Nathan left the house that morning with his sneakers in his backpack, his basketball shorts in his lunch bag, an extra T-shirt folded in his math book, and a plan. He told his mother he was going to the library after school and that Jason Burke's mother was picking them up (so they could do homework), giving him dinner, and bringing him back to the school for a band meeting.

"You can pick me up around seven fifteen . . . no, seven twenty," Nathan told his mom.

"In the back?" she asked. She had Nathan's little sister, as expected, in her arms, pulling on her hair and spitting green baby food on her shoulder. Perfect.

"No," Nathan said. "In the front. It's in the front. Band practice is in the front. That's where the band room is, Mom. God."

"Why didn't you tell me about this meeting before?" she asked.

"Mom, I'm going to be late," Nathan answered. "I did tell you. Last night."

She looked at him.

"Mom. Band is really important to me," he said. But that was a mistake, and as soon as it came out of his mouth he knew it. *Band is really important to me? God, did he really say that?*

There was a pause. Even Nathan's baby sister was silent for a second, as if to show exactly how entirely pitiable that excuse had sounded.

Just then Nathan's dad came into the kitchen.

"Nathan, aren't you going to miss the bus?" his dad asked, and right on cue the baby started screaming, just for no reason. And in the next beat, Nathan's father rolled his eyes like he was really annoyed. He *was* really annoyed. Nathan's father liked things, liked *everything*, a certain way, and that way was neat and quiet. And orderly.

Grades were really important to him. Even shoes were really important to him. Nathan wasn't allowed to wear sneakers to school. A practice virtually unheard of since the early 1960s, nevertheless Nathan had to wear shoes. Real shoes. Or boots. Sandals in the summer. But no sneakers. Sneakers were for the gym only, or better yet, the tennis court.

Nathan's baby sister was now arching her back like a gymnast and flailing her arms around. She caught Nathan's mother in the cheek with a fist. You could tell it took all their mom's strength to hold on to her.

"What's wrong with her?" Nathan's father asked.

"She's a baby." Nathan's mother looked like she might cry. She forgot all about Nathan and his undying love of middle-school band practice.

I might like this kid after all, Nathan thought as he ran out the door.

"'Bye, Mom," he called out. "See you at seven twenty."

Nathan

So it was a bad plan.

It had a million holes in it. What if Nathan's mother called Jason Burke's mother? What if she came early and saw there was no band meeting? What was he going to do from 2:35 dismissal to 5:00, when the basketball clinic started? He'd be hungry.

But it didn't matter. By the time his mother found out, he'd be playing basketball, and at the very worst she'd realize how much he wanted this (he had already convinced himself of this). His sheer determination would be taken into consideration. That would count for something. She'd give in. And then she'd work on Dad. Besides, his mother was mad at his dad for not "ever, ever" helping with the baby. That would certainly work in Nathan's favor.

And what was the problem with playing basketball? What was such a big deal? Didn't Nathan's uncle play professional ball? Didn't he almost make it to the NBA without even going to college? Nathan had never meet his father's brother, but he knew about him. He was a great basketball player. A small forward who could really leap.

However, anything Nathan had been able to find out about his uncle he had to dig for. *Really* dig for. Nathan's father never wanted to talk about it.

Sometimes little pieces slipped out when Grandma Estelle was visiting. Little pieces here and there, over time. Like that fact that Uncle Troy never got to play one minute in the NBA. There was something about violations. And then something about losing a scholarship. Something about a car accident and then drugs. Even something later, long after the basketball dream was vanished, about jail. And now, Nathan knew, Uncle Troy lived somewhere that might as well have been a million miles from North Bridge, and it was unlikely that would ever change.

What Nathan knew most of all was that his father didn't want basketball or anything that had to do with basketball in his life at all.

But that was too bad, wasn't it?

It was just too bad.

Jeremy

Even knowing he wouldn't be staying around much longer, Jeremy hated North Bridge. He hated most of the kids. He hated this clean, shiny gym. Suddenly twenty bucks from his grandmother didn't seem worth it.

He was still standing against the wall when the coaches—at least he figured they were the coaches—

started organizing all the kids. Boys. They were all boys, except for one blonde, skinny girl who had been warming up with everybody else. She had a nasty three-point shot, but when the parents were getting thrown out, she went with them. Jeremy still hadn't touched a ball. He squatted down against the wall. This was so different than he was used to. It was too clean, too new. The lights were on too bright.

There was nothing scribbled on the walls. Not even traces from where someone made you stay after and scrub it off with a brush and a bucket of soapy water. This place was like something on TV, something not real.

And there were so many basketballs rolling all over the place.

Back home there would be twenty or thirty kids and maybe three or four balls. With everyone standing under the hoop waiting for someone else to miss or someone to make it, so they could grab the ball and dribble around a little, pick a good spot, and shoot. Then get into position, maybe yank down a rebound or just wait and hope the ball came your way again.

But here the kids didn't have to wait hardly at all. There were balls flying everywhere. Jeremy had just seen two jerks get hit in the head, there were so many balls. Two balls had actually rolled under the bleachers and nobody even noticed. These kids were so spoiled.

And they sucked.

"You here for the clinic?" Somebody was talking to him.

"Huh?" Jeremy said.

"Are you signed up for the basketball clinic? Are you Jeremy Binder?"

He was one of the coaches. A really tall guy with a clipboard.

"Yes, sir," Jeremy answered.

"Why don't you warm up a little?" The guy smiled. He didn't look so bad. He must have played basketball, if you could imagine him without the big belly and with a lot more hair. Jeez, he was probably seven feet. Anybody could be good at seven feet.

Which made Jeremy think about his father. His father used to tell Jeremy he had some tall genes in the family. Someone way back on his father's father's side was like six-ten or something.

Tall genes skip a generation, you know, Jeremy. A white kid needs all the help he can get.

And then his father would start laughing. He was drinking by then. All the time.

No offense, son, but you ain't no Allen Iverson. You gotta learn to shoot. Like me. Did I ever tell you, Jeremy, I almost made all-state. . . .

Jeremy could remember the story, or less of the

story and more of his father's slurred speech and watery eyes. But he was forgetting how much he hated that. How much it scared him. For some reason, he was forgetting it all.

The tall guy with the clipboard was still standing there, like he wanted something. Like he wanted Jeremy to say something.

But Jeremy had nothing. Nothing to say. Instead he jumped to his feet and ran out onto the court. There was a ball rolling right by.

Perfect.

It fit into his hand. His fingers bent and gripped the leather. Leather, these balls were real leather. He started to dribble without thinking, and everything started to feel better. The sound of the ball bouncing. The rhythm and the bounce. Against the floor and into his hands. Between his legs, back and forth. Behind the back. Dribble. Head up. Ball low.

"Okay, boys let's line up. Balls quiet." It was a different coach. A little short guy with a ridiculous muscle T-shirt and shorts.

Jeremy kept dribbling. Soon his father was gone, the memory was gone, the empty feeling in his chest faded—all he could hear was the ball and the floor and the echo.

"Balls quiet, please."

Jeremy looked up. That little muscle coach was

pissed already. Jeremy held the ball.

"Sorry," Jeremy said.

The tall guy with the clipboard was standing to the side. He nodded his head at Jeremy and smiled.

It's okay, son, he mouthed.

Jeremy lowered his eyes, hoping it looked like he hadn't seen that.

I am so definitely not *your son.*

Hank

The clinics were so stupid. So stupid. It was all drills and suicides; running back and forth; foul line and back, half-court and back, next foul line then full court and back. Hank had come right from soccer, which hadn't been changed after all but had been moved up an hour and a half.

And all that meant for Hank was he had to change out of his cleats and into his basketball stuff in the car. He didn't really have time to eat. His mother had a protein bar for him, but it was disgusting. Raspberry mocha fudge. He took two bites.

The clinic was over. Now it was seven fifteen and he hadn't eaten.

"How was the clinic?" his mother asked him when she picked him up. "How did you do?"

He hated that question. What was he supposed to say?

I did great, Mom. I'm the best one in the whole grade. Just like you and Dad always say: I'm a winner. I've got the eye of the tiger. I'm a natural. The tryout will be a breeze.

What was he supposed to say when she asked him that?

Hank was a very good basketball player. It hadn't been his best day, but it was far from his worst. But how had he been judged this day? The truth was he didn't know. Hank was tired. He played okay. He made some of his shots. Missed more. He had looked around at his competition.

There was a new boy he didn't recognize, but everyone else was pretty much the same. All the kids from last year's fifth grade travel team were there, and a bunch of wannabes. Hank didn't think anything would be different. Except for that new kid.

That kid was good. He was quiet and kept to himself, but he could handle the ball really well, like some of those city kids they had played last year. He always kept his head up and he could dribble through his legs, but not just for show. It was like it was natural to him.

Oh, wait, and Nathan Thomas was there, and he hadn't been there last year. He was okay, but not as good as you'd think. That was kind of funny, Hank thought. Everyone always asked Nathan to play just because he was black. That was some kind of reverse discrimination, wasn't it?

Hank hadn't been listening to his mother, but he knew she had been talking the whole car ride home. Even if he didn't answer his mother, she kept talking. She wanted information so badly she would never let on that she was mad at him. Or that he was rude for not answering.

"So Hank, was Tyler there?"

"Who?" Hank asked.

"Tyler Bischoff."

Hank had to think a minute. Was Tyler there? Yeah, probably. All he could think of was that new kid. What was his name? Hank hadn't even seen him at school before. He started calculating. He had heard they were only taking twelve kids on the team this year. It was sixth grade, and things were going to start to get serious. So if this new kid makes it, who will they cut? Hank's mother was still talking, but somewhere in the last mile or so, her tone of voice had changed. It was squeakier, faster.

"You know, Hank. I take you to school every morning. Take you to soccer. I pick you up from soccer."

What is she talking about?

Hank looked out the window. It was dark, and he still had tons of homework. His legs hurt. He was tired.

He was really hungry.

". . . Take you to basketball. Run back because you forget your Gatorade. Come back and get you."

His mouth was so dry it burned. That's right—his mother had run into the middle of the clinic and waved her arms around to show him where she was placing his Gatorade. She must have seen that he left it in the car, under his soccer stuff and his knapsack. But someone had opened it by mistake (even though his name was all over the side and the lid in black permanent marker) and taken some.

He wasn't about to drink it after that.

"You'd think you'd just say thank you. Just once. Just once, maybe," his mother was saying as they pulled into the driveway.

"Thanks, Mom," Hank said. He hardly had the strength to open the car door.

"Hank?" His mother lowered her voice.

He looked over at her.

"Yeah?"

"I'm sorry," she said.

And he knew she was. She couldn't help it. Hank knew his mother just couldn't stop talking and asking endless questions. Even though the more she pried, the further Hank had to retreat. Hank couldn't change that any more than she could.

Nathan

"This is outrageous. You are definitely going to be grounded."

"He's home now. It's okay."

"How could you do this? How in the hell could you even consider doing this?"

His mother was trying to defend Nathan in between his father's explosive expressions and sound-bite speeches. "He's a boy. He just wants to play. It's just for fun," she was saying.

"Fun?" Nathan's father jumped on that one. "Lying is fun? Scaring everyone half to death is fun? Sneaking around?"

Nathan was quiet. He had been caught. He knew he would be. In fact, he was glad he was. It was inevitable, so it might as well come now. Nathan sat on the couch with his knees pressed together and his arms crossed tightly.

"I don't know what's worse. The sneaking or the lying? Or the lying about the sneaking," Nathan's father shouted. He wasn't making any sense. When

Nathan's father didn't make sense, it wasn't a good sign.

"Don't wake up the baby," his mother shot back.

Nathan's father let out a breath and, it seemed, a little anger with it. He turned to Nathan.

"You lied. You did something you were explicitly told not to do. You had your mother and me worried. And Mrs. Burke, too. You have to be punished."

Nathan nodded. It wasn't that he wanted to be punished. He didn't like being yelled at, either. There was a strength behind his father's rage, a power that was scary but, at the same time, made Nathan angry. Like he wanted to fight back.

"Absolutely no video games for a week," his father said.

"A week?"

"No TV, either."

Nathan didn't look up. His mother would take away the Xbox controllers and hide them, but Nathan knew the No TV would never be enforced. It would last for a day or two, and then his mother would be busy and forget about the whole thing.

Nathan nodded again.

"Do you understand why it's so important that you don't lie to us?"

Nathan's mother spoke softly. It was that soft teacher voice, from when she used to work.

"So you can trust me," Nathan answered.

That seemed to be working. He could practically *feel* it, like something in the air loosening up, dissipating.

"I'm really sorry," Nathan said. "I'm sorry."

It was quiet.

"So you really want to try out for this basketball team?" his father asked him.

"Yeah, Dad, I do."

"Why?"

"I wanna play. My friends are all on the team," Nathan said.

"It's not a goal, you know, Nathan. It's a game. That's all it is. It's not going to lead to anything. It's not going to help you make the right friends or get you into a good school."

So what if his father was wrong about all of the above?

"I know, Dad," Nathan said.

"It's a game."

"I know that, Dad," Nathan said. "It's just for fun. It's healthy, too. It's good exercise. We did a lot of running." He added that one in for his mother.

His father hadn't said yes yet. Nathan wondered what he was thinking. Maybe he was thinking that Nathan would be led down some terrible road to African-American basketball ruin; that his grades would fall off all through high school because all he would do was hang out in the gym and practice ball. He would practically flunk out. But he'd be offered a scholarship at some lousy college anyway. Then he'd get his high-school girlfriend pregnant (not that Nathan had one), get married at eighteen, get injured before he'd had a chance to play, and wind up a strung-out drug addict living on the street.

Is that what his father was thinking?

Is that what had happened to Uncle Troy?

Of course, there was one minor piece of information Nathan's father didn't yet have.

Nathan wasn't good.

In fact, he was probably the worst kid at the entire clinic. He had air balled all his foul shots. He missed all his layups. He couldn't dribble with his left hand at all and not very well with his right. He didn't get one rebound.

"Look at the bright side," Nathan told his father. "I might not even make the team."

His father suddenly stopped thinking and spoke out loud.

"Well, that's nonsense," he said.

Nathan took that as a yes.

THE TRYOUTS

Anabel

For Anabel, her brother's tryout dragged on for two boring hours at the middle school. Her father felt he had to stay, even though all the parents were told it was a closed gym. Apparently her father also felt Anabel was not old enough to stay home alone, and her mother was out of town. Again.

"I could go to Caroline Nagy's house," Anabel begged.

But Caroline Nagy, it turned out, had thrown up three times when she got home from school that afternoon, so Anabel had no other choice but to wait with her father at the tryout. It was too late to call any other friends.

"You can do your homework. You must have

homework," her father suggested. And he left her, with her books sprawled out in the hall floor, while he paced outside the gym doors, which were shut. Every now and then they opened, and one of the coaches or kids stepped out to use the bathroom. When the door stuck open by accident, Anabel's father drifted toward it. For a while he stood in the hall watching, but within a few minutes he was standing inside the gym.

Anabel watched the whole thing. She figured her father would be standing on the sidelines by the locker room within five minutes. Hopefully he'd know enough not to shout out instructions to her brother during the tryout.

"You've got to box out, Michael. Box out!"

Guess not.

She had finished her math and Spanish work. She zipped up her binder. The floor was filthy, and dust had stuck to all her book covers. She sat cross-legged staring at the wall across the way and listening to the balls bouncing inside the gym, like a kind of thunking music. She could hear her father's urgent comments to Michael. Any minute, Anabel predicted, they would be throwing him out of there.

But for the time being, she was alone in the hall. Her mother would call that night and ask if she had done all her homework.

"Yes, Mom," Anabel would say because nothing

less was expected by either of her parents.

School was a sure thing, and Anabel liked that. If you did your work, studied for tests, finished your projects, you were pretty much guaranteed a good grade. There wasn't any risk in that. It was safe.

Anabel thought about her mother packing for her trip that morning.

"Imagine, Annie," her mother was saying. "I was so afraid when I first took this position. I thought I wouldn't be good enough. Nothing was easy. I thought somebody was going to look up from their desk one morning and say, 'Who is this lady? What is she doing here?'"

Her mother laughed. She closed the suitcase and clicked the locks down.

"Sometimes I still feel like that and look, they're flying me all over the country."

"But what if someone does say that?" Anabel asked her mother.

"Say what, honey?" Her mother was pulling the heavy suitcase across the bed. It landed with a thunk on the carpet.

"What if someone says you're not good enough. Says who is this lady? What is she doing here? What would you do then? What *would* you have done?"

Anabel's mother got it all wrong. She thought Anabel was asking her mother about her job. She thought she had needlessly worried her daughter and now she had to comfort her.

"Oh, I was just kidding. I mean, everyone is afraid when they start something new. Right?"

Anabel's mother walked back to the bed. She lifted Anabel's long ponytail of blonde hair and held it in her hands gently.

"I'll be fine," she told her daughter. "Don't worry about me. Everything will be alright."

There was a second Anabel wanted to correct her mother. No, Mom, I meant *me*. I was really asking about *me*. What happens if I try to do something? What happens if I'm not good enough? And what happens if I don't try at all?

But if Anabel had wanted to say something to her mother, she couldn't remember now. Her father came out of the gym with a scowl on his face. That scowl was for Michael, wasn't it?

"I did all my homework, Daddy," Anabel said.

He smiled. "Good girl."

Jeremy

At the end of the tryout, the two coaches—tall with the belly and short with the muscles— came out in the hall to talk to all the parents. The parents stood like they were all holding tickets to the ten-million-dollar lottery drawing.

Jeremy's grandmother wasn't there. She told Jeremy to call her from the pay phone when the tryout was finished. She had had enough experience to know these things never ended on time.

"We will be posting the team roster on the website by Friday night," the tall coach announced.

"What time?" a voice came out of the crowd.

Jeremy made his way over to the pay phone. He dropped in the quarter his grandmother had given him. Then he realized he didn't know his telephone number.

"I don't . . . well, probably by eight o'clock, but I'm not sure how long it takes to go up on the site," the tall coach answered.

"How many players are you taking?" another dad asked.

Jeremy stood with the phone still in his hand. He didn't know what to do.

The two coaches looked at each other as if they had been expecting this question. The muscle coach answered.

"This year we are only taking ten, maybe eleven players."

This caused a gasp in the crowd, followed by a murmur of discontent.

"Why not twelve like last year?" That came from a mom.

Ten was fine, Jeremy thought. There had never had more than ten kids on a team back home. Half the time only two or three parents could drive to the games anyway, and that way everyone could fit into their cars. He was still holding the receiver in his hands.

"The seventh grade had thirteen last year." Another mom.

Thirteen would never fit into two cars. Jeremy put the phone to his ear, but he didn't dial information. It was just as easy to listen to these dumb parents. Obviously the parents who were complaining had kids that sucked. Or they wouldn't be complaining.

The tall coach stepped forward. "We may take twelve. But thirteen is too many. Ten is ideal, with a seven- or eight-man rotation and work in the other two."

Again the crowd shifted around. More people started talking quietly to one another. Jeremy was standing right behind two women and a man who had slipped back a few steps. And they were pissed already.

"Of course, *his* son will make the team. No doubt," the first woman whispered. Loudly.

"Of course. I wonder how many point guards they'll take?" the other woman said.

The man looked at both of them like they were so

totally stupid. "If they only take ten kids, they're not going to take another point guard. Harrison Neeley and Tyler Bischoff both play point," the man said. "Scott doesn't have a chance."

The women both glared at the man.

"You're so negative," the first woman said.

"It's a fact. The two board members' kids make the team, and it's a done deal. Team is filled."

"That's so unfair," the other woman said. She looked like she was going to cry. "Scott is as good as Tyler Bischoff."

"Well, so is Trevor."

The two women agreed. "It's so unfair."

The coaches must have almost finished their talk, because all the parents were gathering up their kids and starting to leave. There was still a lot of talking. The two women had pushed their way, against the flow, up to the two coaches.

"Ten players. Well, we'll just see about that," the first woman was saying to herself. Then Jeremy could see them talking, but he could no longer hear anything clearly. He just wanted to get out of there. He pressed the coin return but his quarter didn't drop out.

"You need a ride?"

Jeremy looked up. It was one of the boys from the tryout. He wasn't bad. Kind of short, but he could handle the ball. And at least he passed the ball.

"Sure," Jeremy said. He hung up the phone. He clicked one more time to see if the coin would come out, but it didn't.

The kid's name was Hank, Jeremy was pretty sure. Yeah, his name was Hank.

Nathan

Nathan watched his father's face when the two coaches talked about how many kids would be making the team and how many kids would be playing.

One of the coaches was answering a question. "Well, let me explain something to you. To everyone. This is sixth grade. And it's travel. If you want to play on a team where everyone gets equal time, then play rec."

Nathan's father was nodding his head. He loved this tough stuff, Nathan knew. He was a self-made man. Nobody had paved his way, nobody had made life easier for him. He didn't ask for favors from anyone and he didn't give them.

"Don't you think they are a little young to make a determination like that?" an anxious woman right up front raised her hand and asked.

She went on, "I think it's too early to be having kids sit on a bench a whole game. They're only eleven and twelve years old."

Nathan's father didn't say anything, but Nathan could see what he thought. *They're old enough. They're old enough to work hard and earn their place.*

"Well, Debbie, that's the league philosophy. You'd have to bring that up with the board," the other coach answered.

The short one had to look up in order to nod his head in agreement when the tall one was talking. Nathan almost started laughing.

When they got into their car, Nathan's father was angry.

"Everyone in this town is looking for the easy way out. They all want the kids to have every advantage. They all think they can get what they want for their kids just by demanding it," Nathan's father was talking.

When his father sounded like this, Nathan always had a picture in his mind of him standing in the laundry room on a box of Tide laundry detergent. That came from the first time his mother told his father to "get down off his soapbox." Even though Nathan had learned what the expression meant, he never could get the image out of his head.

"They are so used to getting their own way," Nathan's father went on. "They've made it to the top, and they think that nothing but the top is good enough for their kids!"

Nathan was used to this. His father went on about this kind of thing all the time. He hated this town and everyone in it. They were all spoiled white elitists. It made Nathan wonder why they had moved here two years ago. His mother hadn't wanted to. Why did his father want him to go to school here?

Who was Nathan supposed to be friends with, if his father disapproved of everyone?

"Some things in life you have to earn," Nathan's father went on. "No matter who you are."

Nathan was quiet.

"I don't have any problem at all with playing the better kids in order to win the game. That's life," Nathan's father said. They were almost home.

"That's life," he said again as they pulled into their driveway. "We won't have any problem with that, will we, Nat?"

"No, sir," Nathan said.

We sure won't have that problem, because there is no way I'm going to be on that team. I lost the ball every time I dribbled. I passed the ball over everyone's head. I dropped every pass. I even kicked the ball once.

But Nathan didn't say that. As angry as his father had been when Nathan had snuck out to the basketball clinic didn't compare to how disappointed he was going to be when he found out his son didn't make the team.

Hank

"So you just moved here?"

Hank hated when his mother did this. It was like she knew that Hank couldn't tell her to stop talking in front of somebody else, so she would take full advantage of the situation and try to extract as much information as she could.

"Yeah," Jeremy answered. He was sitting in the backseat. Hank was in the front.

Thank God his mother hadn't said anything about Hank not exactly weighing enough for the passenger-side air bag. Jeez, that would have been so embarrassing. Almost as embarrassing as having to listen to his mother grill the new boy on where he used to live.

"Oh, that's nice," Hank's mother said. "Do you like it here?"

"I guess so."

"So where did you live before?"

It was so obvious he didn't want to talk about it.

"Central City," Jeremy answered.

That shut her up.

For a second. She just switched topics to her true agenda.

"So how was the tryout? Were there a lot of boys?"

Hank didn't answer, so after a beat Jeremy did.

"About thirty."

"Wow, that's a lot."

"Not really," Jeremy answered.

Jeremy obviously didn't know the secret language of Laurie Adler. Jeremy didn't know what Hank's mother was really trying to find out.

"So . . . how did you two do? Did you play basketball on a team before, Jeremy?"

"Yeah, back home," Jeremy said.

Hank's mother made a little noise like she was trying to sound humbled by that or something. "So how do our North Bridge boys stack up? I mean, what did you think?"

The hidden plan.

"They're okay. Some of them, anyhow."

"Oh," Hank's mother said.

She must have been dying to just come right out and ask, but she didn't have to.

"Hank was definitely one of the good ones. There's no way he won't make the team," Jeremy said.

Maybe he knew that language after all, or maybe Jeremy was just being nice. Or maybe he *was* nice.

Hank shrugged. He turned to Jeremy. "Man, *you're* really good. You were the best one."

Jeremy suddenly laughed. "Hey, did you see that one kid who ducked and put his hands over his head? What was that all about?"

Hank laughed. "Oh, yeah. And did you see the ball bounce off his head and hit that kid, David Sklar, right in the face?"

Just then the car made a sharp left-hand turn. "This is your street, right?" Hank's mother asked. "What number house did you say?"

Hank noticed it. His mother didn't. Jeremy sort of stiffened up and started looking out the window. He didn't know, did he? He didn't know the number of the house.

"There," Jeremy said, pointing. "That house."

"Oh, that's funny. I always thought that was old Nancy Binder's house. You know Nancy? She works at the post office," Hank's mother rattled on.

"It is," Jeremy said quietly.

The car pulled up into the driveway. It was a one-story house with rows of colorful flowers lining the walkway.

"It's my grandmother's house." Jeremy opened the back door and got out. A light in the house went on, like a beacon. "Thanks for the ride, Mrs . . . Thanks."

"Adler. But call me Laurie. And you're very welcome. Any time. We go right by this way" (which they didn't).

"Thanks," Jeremy said.

The door slammed shut. Hank's mother waved to

the woman, who must have been "old Nancy Binder" from the post office, standing at the front door. She did look pretty old.

When they were far enough down the road, Hank looked out the window and said, "Nice going, Mom."

She must have known it, too. She didn't talk the rest of the way home.

North Bridge Sixth-Grade
Travel Basketball Team Roster

(posted on Yourteam.com 8:44 P.M. Friday)

1. Hank Adler
2. Sam Bernegger
3. Jeremy Binder
4. Tyler Bischoff
5. Matt King
6. Scott Brandes
7. Wyatt Greman
8. Michael Morrisey
9. Harrison Neeley
10. Julian Rizzoto
11. Nathan Thomas
12. Camden Tomasello
13. Joey Waterhouse

LET THE SEASON BEGIN

Jeremy

As soon as Jeremy saw the uniforms, he knew this team was going to lose. And it wouldn't be because the uniforms weren't good enough. No, they were nice. Real nice.

It would be for precisely the opposite reason.

The dad of one of the kids brought the huge box into the gym the second day of practice. When he dropped it onto the floor, it made a loud thud. The other kids seemed to know instinctively what was in the box. They all stopped in the middle of their drills and ran over.

Immediately there were the fights over numbers.

"I always get thirty-three."

"So who cares? I want thirty-three."

"Is there four? I want four."

"Let me see. Move, fat ass."

"I want Reggie Miller's number. What's Reggie Miller's number?"

The little muscle coach was guarding the box.

"This will be done fairly," he said. "First everyone needs to take three steps back and sit down."

Everyone took one and a half steps back and sort of sat down. By this time Jeremy had figured there were uniforms in the huge cardboard box. The dad who had brought them in was now laying them out neatly on the floor. Jerseys, shorts, and even matching socks. Jeremy saw what the big deal was all about.

The uniforms were bright, shiny blue with a strip of thick white down the side. On the front of the shirt NORTH BRIDGE was written in a semicircle. On the back was the all-important number. The shorts and the socks were both bright blue with the matching white strip.

Jeremy looked down at the uniforms and around at the kids next to him. He only knew a couple of kids by name. He knew the tall coach was Coach C., which stood for something no one could pronounce. Coach C. didn't seem to have a kid on the team. Jeremy knew the little coach with the muscle T-shirt was this guy Harrison's father, Coach Neeley.

Coach C. said he would call each player up to pick

a uniform one at a time. Alphabetical order.

"But that's not fair."

"Tough," Coach C. answered. He called out the first name, "Hank Adler."

Hank went up and picked number three. Two boys groaned.

"Jeremy Binder," the coach announced.

"Who's Jeremy Binder?"

Somebody pointed when Jeremy stood up.

"Oh." The boy settled back down.

Jeremy walked over to the uniforms lying out like a sale at the NBA store. They were like something he had dreamed of wearing when he made it to the pros. When he was playing for UCLA or Duke. Or Syracuse. When he was dreaming.

"Come on," someone said behind him.

Jeremy bent down and grabbed one of the shirts. Number five. For Jason Kidd.

"Don't forget the shorts. And socks," Coach C. said. He handed Jeremy the rest of his uniform.

"Thanks," Jeremy said.

"And that reminds me," Coach Neeley said. "If you have blue-and-white basketball sneakers, wear them. Or if you are planning on getting new sneakers this season, buy blue ones."

Jeremy looked down at his feet. He had the Jordans. Red and white. There was no way he could ask his grandmother for another pair of sneakers. Anyway, that was stupid.

"We thought it would look good if we all presented ourselves as a unified team for our first game against Walton. It's all about *team*work," Coach Neeley said. Then he repeated his last sentence with the emphasis on the *all* instead of the *team* for some reason. "It's *all* about teamwork."

Teamwork? It would be nice if anyone on this team ever passed the ball. Jeremy knew kids like this back home. When they get a pass, the first thing they do is put it up, no matter where they are standing. Jeremy had never seen so many air balls. Whenever somebody stole the ball, they ran like an escaped convict down the court and missed the easy layup.

Sometimes the guard would just bring down the ball and drive to the hoop without ever passing once. And miss. Over and over again.

Jeremy looked at the silky uniform in his hands. It was soft as butter. It was beautiful, and it was going to give the other team the wrong impression.

No, on second thought, it was going to give the other team the correct impression. Jeremy knew Walton well. Central had played Walton lots of times. North Bridge was going to walk in looking like rich, spoiled kids who think they're hot stuff, and Walton was going to want to kick their asses even more than they were already.

Which is exactly what happened.

Anabel

Anabel's mother was away in Cincinnati when Michael had his first game. She said she felt terrible but it was a big presentation. (It was always a *big* presentation. There were no *little* presentations to Anabel's recollection.)

"Call me from the game," she said as she was leaving. The airport limo had beeped twice from the driveway.

Michael was upset, Anabel knew. He was such a big baby. He ran upstairs and didn't say good-bye. Their mother was supposed to be leaving the next day, but everything got moved up (everything always got moved up). It was worse for Michael that he thought his mother was going to be around than if he hadn't expected it in the first place.

Anabel heard him in his room. The weird thing was how much more it bothered him than Anabel. She was a girl, for heaven's sake, and he was the one crying. And the even weirder thing was she felt bad for Michael.

It was like he was so big and tough and such a great athlete and that was so important to him. It was like, that was who he was. He was Michael, the baseball player and Michael, the basketball player.

So when their mom couldn't come to the game, he was nobody.

And even though Michael picked on her, and punched her in the arm on any occasion, knocked her hat off her head, stole cookies from her lunch bag, and cheated at video games, Anabel loved her brother. She loved him most when she felt bad for him. She decided to go to the game, even though it was a long trip.

Anabel sat in the stands and cheered extra loudly for the whole first half. That was when she noticed a very interesting thing. The parents of the kids who played a lot during the game sat near, or fairly close, to the parents of other kids who played a lot. Their position was near the bottom bleachers, dead center, directly behind the players' bench. So they could shout out instructions.

The parents of kids who played some or a little sat together also, scattered about. They mostly cheered or yelled about bad calls.

But it was the parents of kids who got little or no

playing time at all that made the tightest, most secluded configuration. They sat close to the top, far to the left corner. And they complained. To one another.

Anabel had staked out the top bleachers a long time ago, back when her mother used to come to a game or two. She loved it up there. Her mother said she liked to lean back against the wall. Anabel liked to see the whole court, but no one could see her unless they turned around. But no one ever did. Most of the grown-ups didn't like climbing so high. It was her spot, and that's where she was sitting at Michael's first game that year.

When all of a sudden, this old lady came up.

This old lady who had been sitting on the other team's bleachers for the whole first half of the game. At halftime when all the parents got up to stretch their legs or go to the bathroom, this old lady made her way all the way up to the top bleacher and sat down right next to Anabel.

"Well," the lady said, plopping herself down on the seat. "That was a long way up."

Anabel wasn't thrilled by the intrusion into her sacred space, but she was curious about who this lady was and why she had come from the other side to sit here.

"I guess I was on the wrong side, the whole time,"

the lady explained, although Anabel had never asked. "That is, if you think there is a right or a wrong side."

"Well, this is the North Bridge side," Anabel said. "Are you rooting for North Bridge or Walton?"

"I suppose I am. North Bridge, I mean," the lady said. "My grandson is on this team."

A very loud buzzer sounded to end halftime, and the referees called the teams to the floor. The lady looked around.

"The crowd seemed happier on the other side," she said.

"That's because they're winning," Anabel told her.

The lady laughed. She had a nice smile. She was a little fat and very gray. She was wearing ugly, stretchy pants and a too-colorful sweater. Anabel thought she looked familiar, too, but she couldn't figure out from where.

"The other team must be pretty good," the lady said.

"No, we're just terrible," Anabel said. Then she remembered. This was the lady from the post office. "We don't play like a team. Every kid out there thinks he's the best because that's what his father told him. Nobody looks to pass. They just get the ball and shoot. Not one kid has set a pick. See that big kid, Joey?"

The lady nodded like she was really listening. Anabel thought it was nice to have someone to talk to again.

"The first rebound he got he just put it right back up."

"That's good, isn't it?"

"It was the other team's basket."

The lady laughed again. She was an easy laugh. "Oh, yes. I saw that. At least he got it in."

Anabel laughed, too. It *was* funny, in a pathetic sort of way.

"You know a lot about basketball," the lady said.

"I watch it a lot on TV," Anabel explained.

"You must play, too. I bet you're really good," the lady went on. "I can just tell."

Anabel looked down at Michael. He was sitting on the bench, slouched down. He had kicked the bench when the coach called him in. He had just missed the last three shots he had taken. He had looked up at their dad each time. Anabel could just sense how awful he must feel.

"No," Anabel said. "I don't play."

Hank

Since it had been an away game, the boys had to use the Walton girls' locker room. The parents all waited in the lobby outside the gym. Slowly the boys trickled out of the other locker room door down the hall. Hank felt bad enough that they had lost their first game. He didn't want to hear his dad's interpretation. He really didn't. But he couldn't help it. His dad was talking to the other dads pretty loud.

"That coach doesn't know the first thing about defense. Look how he positioned those kids."

They had lost so badly. 54–21.

"He never had the right combination of kids out there," Tyler Bischoff's dad was saying.

"What credentials does this Coach C. have anyway?" Mr. King added in. His son Matt also played Pop Warner. Matt was one of those boys who was so big for his age that if he hadn't played football, you would wonder why not.

"Who hired him?" Hank's mother asked. "Oh, the boys are out." She waved. "Hank, over here."

Hank walked hanging his head. His eyes were rimmed in red. As soon as he got into the car, it surprised him, but he started to cry.

"What did that coach say to you?" his mother demanded.

"Nothing," Hank said.

"Why are you so upset?" his father asked. He was trying to reverse the directions he had printed out from the computer and get them home.

"Because I suck," Hank shouted. He felt like shouting.

"You do not," his mother said. She turned around from the front seat to look at him. "You're a great player." Her voice turned soft.

"Don't talk to me!" Hank yelled.

"You've just got to shoot the ball more," his father said. He made a right turn into someone's driveway and backed up to turn around. He had gone the wrong way. "You're too tentative. You've got to shoot more."

"The coach told us to pass more, so shut up," Hank said. He didn't even get in trouble for saying that.

Instead Hank's mother and father looked at each other knowingly. Hank was a good athlete. A great athlete, wouldn't you say? He had instincts. He was quick. He knew the game. It was obvious that poor coaching was at fault here.

Nathan

Nathan's parents didn't come to the game. Nathan's dad had too much work to do and was doing a pretty good job of trying to pretend basketball didn't matter to him. Nathan's mother thought the baby would just be so difficult that she wouldn't get to sit and watch.

So his mother had gotten Nathan a ride with Wyatt Greman, who happened to live on the same street. Driving home from the game Wyatt's parents were whispering, but what was the point? Wyatt and Nathan were sitting in the third seat of their huge Suburban. And the radio was on.

Nathan couldn't hear what they were saying, but he didn't have to. Wyatt hadn't gotten off the bench more than three times (two more times than Nathan), and then only for about one minute. He lost the ball both times he came down the court. The coach pulled him and put Tyler Bischoff back in. At least Tyler got past half-court.

Then they lost possession.

Wyatt's parents were clearly upset. Their voices got louder just as the radio DJ decided to play a slow, quiet song.

"How can you expect a kid to sit for half an hour

and then jump up and be warmed and ready?"

"You know, Michael Morrisey played the whole game. I don't think he sat once."

"And Michael missed five baskets in the first quarter."

"Who *is* this coach?"

"Well, Neeley's dad is the assistant. That explains that."

"So who is the head coach? That tall guy. Who hired him?"

"I don't know. Nobody asked us."

Wyatt looked embarrassed, but he didn't say anything. There were earphones plugged into an outlet in the backseat. He put them on. He pointed to another pair on Nathan's side.

Grateful, Nathan pressed the headset over his ears. Wyatt pushed a button and a small TV slowly opened from the console in the center ceiling of the car. It was about a forty-five minute ride back to North Bridge. Nathan tried to forget about the game. He was pretty confident no one had really noticed how bad he was.

The movie began. The film credits rolled across the tiny screen.

The game had been a big mess, really. No matter what the coach had told them to do, when each player got onto the court he dribbled the ball (the coach told them not to dribble), never passed (the coach told them to pass right away), and shot (the coach said not to shoot until they had had at least three passes). It was a disaster. And it was noisy. You could hear Coach C. yelling from the bench.

"Pass. Pass the ball!"

And you could hear the referee, blowing his whistle and trying to help a little with some instructions.

"You can't pull his shirt, son. Next time that's a foul."

You could hear the dads shouting from the bleachers.

"Shoot."

"Shoot the ball, Sam."

"Take the shot, Tyler!"

"Drive in, Hank. Drive in."

"Matt, you're wide open, just shoot!"

The moms seemed more interested in defense.

"Hands up!"

"Hands up!"

"Watch out!"

"Oh, no."

And, of course, the other team trash-talking the whole time. Nobody heard that but the boys on the court. Kids do it all the time. If you're really good at it, nobody hears but the kid right next to you. Those

Walton kids were real good at it.

"Rich boy, you couldn't hold onto that ball with superglue."

"Nice uniform, preppy."

"Rich kids can't even buy a basket."

And under their breath when they thought no one else could hear, "Even their black kid can't play ball."

There were two black kids on Walton's team. One was real tall, real skinny, and real good. He scored most of the fifty-four points for their team. The other kid was very dark skinned and kind of chubby. He didn't play much. His glasses got knocked off his face in the first few minutes of the game, and he mostly sat with ice on his nose.

Nathan was glad it was over. He was glad nobody had gotten him the ball. He was glad it wasn't a close game so it hadn't have mattered when his inbounds pass was intercepted by a kid on the other team. He was glad it was such an awful game that nobody would really wonder why he had gotten picked for the team.

Nathan wondered.

But mostly he was glad his father hadn't been there.

FLAGRANT

*C*oach C. was fired. Well, not fired exactly, since he wasn't getting paid in the first place. He was a nonparent volunteer, and he got unvolunteered after the first game. What followed was a semi-democratic hostile takeover.

An emergency meeting was held in the North Bridge Public Library community room. The Gremans were thrilled. The Neeleys said, a bit too casually, that they didn't care one way or the other. In fact, Mr. Neeley would remain assistant coach either way.

Dan Morrisey, Michael's dad, was furious. He thought Coach C. had done "a damn good job, considering what he had to work with." Camden's parents thought Coach C. was a little too rough for kids that age. The Waterhouses thought it was too early to tell. Nathan's father was at work. His mother showed up but was in the bathroom changing a poopy diaper when the crucial vote was taken.

The minirevolution was staged and the coup carried out. Coach C. was history.

BOUNCE PASS

Joel Bischoff and Coach Neeley ran the practices for the next couple of weeks. Sam Bernegger's mother worked over at the university, and she said she'd put up a notice for a new coach. A paid coach. Maybe a physical education major or just one of those sports-crazy young students would be interested.

What they got wasn't a phys ed major or even a student exactly, but Duke Hand *was* crazy. He had taken a couple of undergraduate classes that semester and he saw the posting. He wanted to someday "major in law" so he could become a sports agent and make a lot of money. The North Bridge parents had another meeting, and they even agreed to pay the little extra for Coach Hand's transportation costs.

Nathan

Nathan had never known a grown-up who cursed like Coach Hand did, not in public, anyway. It was kind of exciting, like all of a sudden being in a movie that his mother would never have let him see. And being that he was sitting on the bench for the entire North Bridge vs. Strathmore game, Nathan got to hear it all.

"One of these home games, I'll come to," Nathan's father had told him that morning.

This was when Nathan acted all hurt and he pretended to beg his father. It was the reverse-psychology manipulation. And it was working.

"C'mon, Dad. You'll love it. It's real exciting."

"If you were really doing it just for fun, it wouldn't matter if I came to watch or not," his father said. "You don't ask me to watch you play computer games, do you? You don't want me to cheer you on when you're playing GameBoy?"

"No," Nathan answered.

"This whole sports thing is out of control. It's not about the kids anymore," Nathan's father said. He got up from the table to clear his breakfast dishes. "Maybe it never was."

Nathan watched his dad. All these weeks he had come home from practices and told his dad about the scrimmages and about the other players. Mostly he told his dad about Jeremy, about how he made the shot in the final seconds, or how Jeremy had stuffed some kid just as he was about to make a crucial layup. He told his dad about how Jeremy never lost the ball and could dribble between his legs.

Only when Nathan told the story, *he* was Jeremy.

His father never seemed to notice. At first Nathan was certain his father would realize these stories of amazing feats of athletic ability couldn't be about his son. But he didn't. And the stories just got bigger.

And bigger.

His father just listened, as if he had expected Nathan to be some great basketball star all along, just like everybody else had. Only he wasn't. Being black may have gotten Nathan on the team, but it didn't get him onto the floor. After the first couple of practices, it was obvious he never should have made the team.

Of course, nobody said that.

Nobody even seemed to believe it. Nathan just kept puttering along, missing layups and double dribbling. When they got to the game, he pretty much sat on the bench. At that last game, it had turned out to be the best seat in the house.

FADEAWAY JUMP SHOT

*C*oach Hand argued every call. He even argued the jump ball to start the game. He said that the referee threw the ball closer to the kid on the other team. At first the referee was nice about it.

"Coach, you got possession. What are you complaining about?"

But about two minutes into the first half and twenty comments later, the referee started to lose his temper.

"Call the foul, ref!" Coach Hand yelled. "I could hear that slap from here."

Matt King had lost the ball coming downcourt. The referee said it was clean, but Coach Hand didn't agree. It didn't help that the North Bridge parents seemed to be fueling Coach Hand's paranoia.

"What horrible reffing," Hank Adler's dad called out from the bleachers.

Coach Hand stood up in full agreement with that assessment.

"Sit down, coach," the referee said. "This is a warning."

Coach Hand yelled back, "Just call it both ways."

The referees gave him a look and then began the play again. This time it was Tyler Bischoff going in for a layup and missing the shot.

"That was a foul," Coach Hand stood up and screamed.

This time the referee blew his whistle. He made the shape of a T with his hands, a technical foul. Coach Hand went crazy. The parents did, too.

"What?" Tyler's dad shouted from the bleachers. "What kind of call is that?"

The referee went over to the bleachers. He pointed right at Tyler's dad. "Look," he said. "I've got a certificate and rule book in my car. Do you want to see them?"

"Yeah, well. I got a pair of glasses and a whistle in my car, wanna use *them*?" Tyler's dad shouted back.

The referee made the big T with his hands again. That's when Michael Morrisey's dad stood up. "You can't T up a parent!"

"I just did," the referee answered. "That's four shots for Strathmore." He blew his whistle extra long and loud. But it wasn't over.

It was *not* over.

Not before Coach Hand let fly a combination of four-letter words that most of the boys had never even heard before; some configurations of people and animals and curse words that defied the imagination. Even the North Bridge parents got quiet. Everyone was looking at Coach Hand, who didn't seem to notice. He still seemed to feel the power of the mob that was no longer behind him.

That's when it ended.

The coach was asked to leave. Actually the referee threw him out of the game and Harrison Neeley's dad (speaking for everyone involved) asked Duke Hand not to come to the next practice.

North Bridge lost 63–28.

Jeremy

Jeremy went straight up to his room after the game. His grandmother hadn't been able to go this time. She had to work. She had tried to change her schedule with someone else at the post office, but that person had a doctor's appointment and, well, Jeremy's grandmother was sorry. Jeremy knew she really was.

She wasn't home yet, and Jeremy was kind of glad. He didn't feel like telling her about the game. He didn't even care. He barely got to play. But it wouldn't have made much difference.

Jeremy sat down on his bed. On *the* bed. It wasn't his. Not really. His grandmother said it had been his father's room, though you'd never have been able to tell. There was no evidence of this having once been anyone's bedroom, except for the bed. It looked like the room had been used as storage for about a hundred years. His grandmother had tried to clean it out as best she could (she bought him a new comforter), but there just wasn't a place for all of this stuff. Pictures, boxes, folded blankets, old clothes, smelly books, smelly magazines, a bag of extension cords. A bag of bags. His grandmother didn't throw much away. She just put things in bags and pushed them into the corners.

So this had been his father's room. Jeremy looked around at the walls. They were dark-paneled wood, or fake wood maybe. He couldn't tell.

And so this was the town that his father had grown up in. Weird. Totally weird. Everyone here was so fancy and rich. Nothing like his father. Or nothing like what he remembered of his father.

What did he remember about his father? He hadn't seen him in almost six months. Jeremy knew that after his mother died, the woman in the next apartment started baby-sitting. It wasn't Lannie. It was two or three someones before Lannie. Jeremy was only five, but he remembered it didn't feel right that the baby-sitter starting staying with them even when his father came home from work.

Jeremy did remember his father's mother, his grandmother, coming to visit sometimes. She always brought presents, and Jeremy liked that. But his father didn't. You could just feel it. Something was wrong. They didn't like each other. His dad didn't like Jeremy's grandmother and Jeremy's grandmother *really* didn't like the baby-sitters. Any of them.

Jeremy kicked off his sneakers. One slid onto the floor and the other one went the other way, against the wall. It knocked into a little green-painted frame hanging sort of cockeyed, almost completely hidden by a tall cardboard box. It was the only thing in the room that looked like someone had once put it there on purpose. Someone had bought that cheery green frame and framed whatever was under that glass.

Jeremy leaned off the bed to read it.

North Bridge High School
North Bridge, Connecticut
Having met the requirements for graduation
as prescribed for the senior high school
by the Board of Education
of the township of North Bridge

Ronald Binder

is hereby declared entitled to all the privileges
belonging to a graduate of this school and
in recognition thereof is awarded this

Diploma
Twenty-first day of June 1985

It was his father's diploma, still hanging on the wall. Framed. Well, so here was definite proof that this had been his father's room. His father really had lived here. Gone to school here. Slept in this room. Studied. Maybe talked on the phone to his friends.

And all of a sudden something jumped into Jeremy's brain. Something from the game that afternoon. It was after Coach Hand had gotten kicked out and they started the game again. The team was down by a million and two points. There was no chance of even coming close. The coach called Jeremy and a bunch of other kids off the bench. He went in with the loser team.

He didn't care.

There was a minute and a half left on the clock. Jeremy stole the ball. He'd passed it to that big kid, Joey Water-something, and by some miracle he caught it. Jeremy dodged inside. He didn't look. He knew it, the ball was coming back to him. The big kid bounced the ball back, and Jeremy snagged it down low. He dribbled two times hard, between two kids on the other team who were closing in on him. It was like slow motion. He went up. The ball rolled off the tip of his fingers and through the net, and then, out of the corner of his eye, Jeremy thought he saw him. He thought he saw his father. Was that him? Or someone who looked like him?

Forty-five seconds left.

He really did. It was as if his father was there. Watching him. So proud.

It felt like energy inside. It felt, for those few seconds, like everything was all right again. The other team scored, and on North Bridge's next possession Jeremy came downcourt, caught the ball at the three-point line, and hit the shot.

He was sure someone was watching him. But when the buzzer sounded to end the game, Jeremy looked again. No one was there.

POST UP

Two days later Coach Vince was hired and Harrison Neeley's dad was demoted to scorekeeper. Although it wasn't called a demotion. It's just that in an effort to be 100 percent fair there really shouldn't be any parents on the bench during games. If there are no parents coaching, then no one can accuse anyone else of playing favorites. An objective, honest, qualified coach was needed once more. And Coach Vince accepted.

It seemed just right. Vince Anderson had played high school and college basketball. He had coached at the Y and the Boys and Girls Club in New York, where he was from. He was married only a few years and had no children yet. He worked during the day and his wife worked late. He loved basketball and he loved kids.

No, he didn't want to get paid. It was like a hobby. He liked being part of the community.

Everyone had a good feeling. The kids liked him right away.

And in a stroke of fortune or misfortune, depending on your point of view, Sam Bernegger's dad said he could get all the boys leather basketball jackets from a friend of his, wholesale. Jackets with their names on the back. They needed a boost; after all, there was still more than three-quarters of the season to go. What's eighty-five dollars?

A bargain.

SECOND HALF

Hank

Hank loved being on the travel team. There was something about everybody being on the same side, wanting the same thing, and fighting the same enemy; something that never happened in school or anywhere else. So in spite of having gone through three coaches already (if you include the two dads who took over for a short time), in spite of the fact that they were zero and five, and that they were nothing but a huge embarrassment to the North Bridge basketball board, Hank loved being on the team.

He wore his team jacket to school. Proudly.

"Hey, Adler, why don't your jackets just say *loser* on the back."

Hank put his lunch tray on the table. There were

five crucial minutes or so when the seventh-graders were passing through from recess and sixth-grade lunch began. Hank wished he had taken a minute or so longer at the counter.

Hank turned around, even though he knew better. Even though he knew the owner of that voice was Alex Lyons; Alex, who had been picking on Hank since the beginning of this year, since sixth-graders started riding the middle-school bus. There was no real explanation for it. There had never been an original fight or disagreement. Never once had Hank said anything or done anything to make Alex Lyons decide to pick on him and nobody else.

It was just one of those things. One of those being in the wrong place at the wrong time kind of things.

Hank's mother never understood. The same way his parents never understood why Hank wasn't always a starter on the basketball team. They were certain it was all political. Another conspiracy.

"Well, it must have been something," his mother said. "Can't you talk to this Alex boy? What's his last name? I'll call his mother. I'll call the bus driver."

That was the first and *last* time Hank told his mother about Alex Lyons. And some days were better than others. Some days Alex wasn't in the mood and didn't say anything when Hank got on the bus or saw him in school. And some days were like today.

"Your team sucks it up big-time. The rec team is better. And I hear you haven't made a shot the whole season," Alex said.

"You got the fancy jacket and all your ass is doing is collecting splinters."

That was Alex's friend, Carter Bunnell.

"Why don't you sell the jacket and take some shooting lessons?" Alex laughed. "Not that it would help. Lo-ser." He made an L shape and held it up to his forehead.

Hank still had not said anything.

Alex Lyons wasn't that big. But Carter Bunnell was huge. Huge and majorly ugly. Everyone knew Carter had beat up an eighth-grader at the beginning of this year for picking up his backpack by mistake. Both Carter and Alex played on the seventh-grade travel basketball team.

Carter already had lots of hair under his arms, and Alex was developing acne.

"Why don't you see if the girl's team has an opening," Carter said, walking past.

"Yeah, keeping the score book," Alex said, and as he walked past he shoved Hank with his shoulder. It was the first time he had actually touched Hank. Hard.

Hank reeled around and pushed Alex in the back.

It happened so fast. The strength of his own reaction surprised Hank. It was an instinct he didn't know he had.

"Go to hell," Hank added in, because at this point, why the hell not?

By now more than a few kids in the cafeteria had noticed and started forming a kind of spontaneous circle. For the briefest second Hank was reminded of a picture in his social studies book: cavemen moving in for the big kill, surrounding one poor defenseless buffalo.

"You little turd," Alex said, and spun back around. Carter immediately stepped up beside him.

So this is it.

This is a fight. Hank's heart started beating wildly. He was caught between pure fear and an incredible anger that was rising inside of him, as if it had been waiting there every bus ride of every morning all year. Hank felt his mouth go dry instantly. His fingers were tingling and his knees felt like rubber, like after running the mile in gym class. Apparently fear had some side effects.

He could only hope that his anger would give him superhuman powers (he was going to need them), like in that movie from health class that showed how the fight-or-flight part of your brain sends out a message to release lots of adrenaline.

Hank was hoping lots of adrenaline makes you *really*, really strong.

Or that the cafeteria lady (hurry up, please) would come rushing over and break it up.

But instead, something more remarkable happened.

"Leave him alone, asshole."

It was Jeremy Binder.

Anabel

Anabel saw the whole thing. She was sitting with Brigit and Erin, her two best friends. She watched until that new boy, Jeremy, suddenly jumped up and rushed all the way over from the other side of the cafeteria to where Hank Adler was standing. Normally somebody rushing, even somebody running, wouldn't seem so unusual, but there was something so deliberate about Jeremy's motion. Anabel thought she could sense a change in the actual atmosphere in the room. And even though she really had never seen it before, Anabel knew something very aggressively boylike was about to happen.

"What's going on?" Erin said. She was just about to take everything out of her lunch bag.

"Looks like a fight," Brigit said. "That new boy

just ran over there like he was going to hit some-body."

"Jeremy Binder," Anabel said.

"You know him?" Brigit asked.

"He's on my brother's basketball team."

"He's cute," Erin said.

"Yeah, and he's going to be killed," Brigit added. "That's Carter and Alex over there. It's going to be terrible." She stood up. "Let's go watch."

Erin and Anabel didn't hesitate.

It's just that there were not many good fights in North Bridge. Not any at all, really. Just the occa-sional shoving, pushing, name-calling, send everyone to the principal's office. Last year a kid got in trouble for stealing another kid's Palm Pilot from the gym lockers. And of course there was a rumor that Carter Bunnell beat up an eighth-grader who had cut in front of him in the lunch line. But Anabel had never talked to anyone who had really *seen* that themselves. Or even knew who the eighth-grader was. Only half the kids believed it happened at all. The other half had a completely different story about a backpack or something like that.

Not that she didn't think it was possible. Boys do all sorts of weird stuff. Having an older brother at home gave Anabel special insight. Hitting, farting, grabbing, running, burping, kicking, tripping, cursing, all seemed to be male favorites. Reciting lines from stupid movies was right up there.

But fighting ranked high.

By the time Anabel, Erin, and Brigit made their way into the circle, the fight was over. You could tell nothing had happened. It was a standoff, a name-calling flop fight. At least, that's what all the kids were saying as they began to wander away.

"Everybody go back and sit down," Mrs. Ossie, the cafeteria lady said. She had one hand on Carter's shoulder.

But Anabel saw something else. She saw Jeremy standing next to Hank, right next to him, for no other reason than they were on the same team. Jeremy probably didn't even know Carter. Or Alex. He probably had no reason in the world to get into a fight with either of them (although something told Anabel that if there *had* been a fight, Jeremy would have won it).

But there he was. No questions asked. Jeremy had come from all the way on the other side of the cafeteria to take Hank's side. To be *on* his side.

Hank knew it, too. You could see it in the way he was standing.

And when she recognized it, Anabel was suddenly envious.

Jeremy

Jeremy's back was starting to hurt from sitting slouched down in the chair outside the assistant principal's office for so long. He was about to sit up, straightening out his back for a little relief, but he looked over at Hank. Hank had his legs out, his hands in his jean pockets, and his butt at the very end of the upholstered chair, too, so Jeremy decided to stay down. He could ignore the aching in his back. It wasn't worth looking eager or too concerned.

Mr. Bernardino's door could open any minute.

One of those boys, Alex or Carter, had already been in there and was gone. The other one, Jeremy didn't know which was which, was still in there. Jeremy had heard the assistant principal call their names, like he knew them already. Pretty well.

Alex and Carter. No tough guys are named Alex and Carter.

"You didn't have to do that."

He turned to the sound of Hank's voice. "Do what?" Jeremy asked.

"I mean, you didn't have to get in trouble. For me," Hank explained.

Jeremy didn't say anything. His back hurt too

much, and Jeremy shifted his legs in and sat up.

Hank immediately did the same. "But thanks," he said.

They were quiet again for a long while, still waiting, staring straight ahead. They could hear a deep, muffled voice on the other side of the wooden door. Obviously Mr. Bernardino was doing all the talking. It's always that way. Jeremy wasn't planning on saying anything when it was his turn. Nothing at all.

"We have two games this weekend."

"Huh?"

"Saturday and Sunday. We have two games," Hank said. "If you need a ride or anything."

Why would he think that? Why would he think I don't have a ride, Jeremy thought. Like it's written all over my face. Like my grandmother can't drive a car or something?

Jeremy turned to say something appropriate and then stopped. Hank didn't really mean anything by that. He probably just wanted to be friends. Hank was pretty okay, and he was a pretty good basketball player, too.

"I'll let you know," Jeremy answered.

The sound of a chair scraping against the floor and heavy footsteps meant Bernardino must be done with that big kid, Alex or Carter. Whichever one was the real big kid with the blonde hair.

"He wouldn't have done anything," Jeremy told Hank.

"Who?"

"That big kid." Jeremy pointed to the door.

"Oh, you don't know him," Hank said, shaking his head.

The door opened and Carter Burnell hurried out. He took up a lot of space. Jeremy and Hank watched him go. Mr. Bernardino called Hank in. Jeremy slouched down even further in his seat and waited.

Anabel

Normally Anabel wasn't crazy about old people. It wasn't like there were really any in her family. Both sets of her parent's parents had died years ago. She didn't even have a very old teacher. Mrs. Fronheiser in elementary school was pretty old, like fifty or something. But Jeremy's grandmother, Mrs. Binder, was probably the oldest person Anabel had been this close to.

It wasn't really that she didn't *like* old people, but they seemed *so* old. So far away from understanding anything Anabel was thinking or doing. And they look different.

Anabel had watched her mother looking in the mirror, putting on her makeup, getting ready for work.

"My lids are sagging. Anabel, look. Didn't they used to be here?" she said. She had her pointer finger tugging up at her eyes.

Anabel was sitting on the side of the bathtub. "No. You look exactly the same. You look beautiful," she said.

Anabel's mother didn't put down her mascara, but she turned sideways and kept jerking the little black wand up at her lashes. "You're sweet," she said.

She looked back into the mirror. "But, God. I'm getting old. Life is too short. You know that, Ana? That's why you've got to make the most of it. It just goes by so fast."

Anabel didn't answer. Life might be short, but some days were really, really long. Besides, even as her mother was telling her to make the most out of life, Anabel knew she couldn't. She wouldn't. It was very comforting to do the exact same thing every day, doing only what you know you are good at.

There was also something comforting about Mrs. Binder, even though *her* eyelids had clearly sagged completely years ago.

"Your brother just made a shot," Mrs. Binder told Anabel. She pointed down to the court.

They had a ritual. They always climbed up to the top bleacher, far to the left, and leaned their backs against the wall. Mrs. Binder brought homemade cookies and Anabel brought two extra juice boxes from her pantry.

"It was a lucky shot," Anabel said. She poked the ministraw into her juice box.

"Oh, you're too hard on him. He's good. Look, he just tried to block that other boy from shooting."

"He fouled him," Anabel said.

"Is that bad?"

And she kind of liked that Mrs. Binder didn't know anything.

"It means the other team not only gets the two points, but they get to shoot a foul shot," Anabel explained.

"Oh, that's bad then."

"Right."

It was getting crowded on the bleachers. The teams for the next game were starting to arrive and, of course, their parents. Some of the North Bridge parents moved up to see better.

It was a close game. This new coach was doing a pretty good job. He had gotten all of the kids to play at least a little, and he put the weaker kids in with the stronger players so everyone looked better.

Anabel was surprised. They might even win this

game. Jeremy was playing great. Anabel was just about to tell that to Mrs. Binder, but two of the dads sat down right in front of them, nearly right on her feet.

"Who found this guy?" one of the dads was saying. Anabel thought it was Tyler Bischoff's dad, but she wasn't sure.

"I think Bruce Adler did. I think he knew someone who knew someone at his office," the other dad answered.

"Well, that explains that."

"What? Adler playing the whole game?"

"Yeah, and look at that new kid, Binder. What a ball hog. He never passes."

Anabel looked over to Mrs. Binder to see if she had heard. It was hard to tell. She was just watching the game. She just rooted for everyone. Every kid. She even clapped when the other team made a basket.

The-maybe-Tyler's-dad-guy leaned in closer to the other man. "Wyatt is open half the time, but that kid never gets him the ball. He just shoots."

So that was Wyatt Greman's dad. Anabel knew his little sister, Caroline, from Girl Scouts two years ago. She watched Mr. Greman's bald head nodding in agreement.

"He plays street ball. It looks good now, but against a good team he'll turn over the ball every time."

That is so not true, Anabel thought. Jeremy was better than both their kids combined and they just didn't like it. Anabel didn't want to look over at Mrs. Binder again. Hopefully she didn't understand what they were talking about. Or she didn't know they were talking about her grandson. Or at best, she didn't know they were saying mean things about him.

The game was finally over. North Bridge won 36–33. The boys were jumping all over one another. Everyone looked really happy. Except for Mrs. Binder. She didn't say anything to Anabel. She didn't even say her usual, "Oh, Anabel, you'll be playing someday. And you're going to knock 'em all off their feet."

Anabel figured that even if she hadn't heard what those dads were saying, she could *feel* it. It was ugly. Like toxic waste.

Mrs. Binder made her way slowly down the bleachers. Anabel watched her as she waited for Jeremy. She tried to put her arm around him when they were walking out, but he wouldn't let her.

It was like she was trying to protect him from that feeling. But Mrs. Binder had no idea what she was up against. She just had no idea.

But Anabel did.

Nathan

Nathan's father was excited to hear about the win. So perhaps, Nathan thought later, he had talked it up *too* much.

The new coach, Quince or Vince or whatever, told everyone at halftime that the team needed a win this time. He said the play was going to be to Jeremy. He told Julian and Matt where to stand to set picks and keep the lane open. He told Camden to keep getting those offensive rebounds. He told Hank to keep pressing their point guard. It was working great. And he told Jeremy to keep shooting. He was hot.

When you're hot, shoot, he told Jeremy.

Winning was good, Nathan thought. Even though he barely got off the bench the whole time, it was better than losing. It felt good. Satisfying.

No, it was fantastic.

And it made a much better story. Nathan's mother had made roast turkey breast with gravy, string beans, and sweet potatoes. It all felt very festive.

"I think I might like to come to your next game," his father said. "Against Hollis. Is that right? It's an away game, isn't it?"

"Huh?" Nathan stopped his fork midway to his mouth.

"I want to try out our new digital camera," his

father added. "It's got a telephoto lens, you know."

"I'll come, too," his mother said. She was smiling, but she had it all wrong, Nathan thought. He knew she was feeling guilty about the new baby taking up so much of her time. And true, Nathan hadn't done much to convince her otherwise.

"No, that's okay, Mom," Nathan said. "I know how tired you are."

He wasn't going to be able to reverse the damage now. He had made it all sound so great. He had gotten carried away.

"Of course I'm not too tired," she said. "I want to see my son play."

Didn't they say there was an amino acid in turkey that made people relax and feel good? Tryptophan, that was it. Only Nathan wasn't feeling too good right then.

"Maybe we won't win again," Nathan tried. "Maybe never again."

"So what?" his father said. He pushed his seat back from the table. He was actually smiling. It was definitely the tryptophan. It produced serotonin, which affected the part of the brain involved in relaxation.

"But I might not play much this time," Nathan went on. "I mean, since I played so much last game. You know, it's got to be fair and all."

"I think the coach will play the best players. You're

not babies. You're in sixth grade. In three years you'll be in high school. At some point you play to win," his father was saying. "The better players play more. You kids have to learn that sometime."

Nathan wondered what planet his father had been living on.

"At least athletics is the one place where fair is fair. Where the better man gets the job," Nathan's father went on.

He had spent so much of his life working hard. He had three graduate degrees that Nathan knew of. His father had so left behind the world he had come from, but he hadn't quite landed in this one. Sports wasn't fair at all. Fathers favored their own kids. Coaches had one agenda. Parents had another. Some kids made the team even when there were other kids who were clearly better. Some parents did favors for the coach; others just complained really loud.

But Coach Vince seemed pretty fair. Everybody played. And besides, they won. Nathan almost smiled again, remembering, and then his mother spoke.

"Anyway, it doesn't matter if you play a lot," his mother said. "We'll just come to root for your team."

Mothers.

"It's settled then," Nathan's father said.

Nathan thought he might be allergic to serotonin.

Hank

"It's school policy not to ask anyone why they're in here," Mrs. Cooperman said. She was in charge of detention that day.

"So why are you in here?" she asked.

Hank smiled right away. Mrs. Cooperman was pretty and funny. Maybe detention wouldn't be so awful after all.

The whole thing had made him pretty nervous. He had never really *had* detention before. Not a real stay-after-school kind of detention. He had a bad stomachache that morning. He didn't even want to go to school. But he had to. The school had called his mother the day before and sent him home with a note. Two days of detention.

There is a no-tolerance rule about fighting, Hank's mother was informed. (Of course, she called right away.) It didn't matter who started it or for how long this boy, Alex, had been picking on her son. Hank's mother almost started to cry right on the phone with the assistant principal. (*Oh, God, please no.*) Not because she thought Hank had been hurt, he obviously wasn't hurt, but for the injustice of it all.

Hank's parents had this thing about injustice.

"It was no big deal," Hank had tried to explain that night.

"Well, I'm glad you stood up for yourself," Hank's dad said. "You should do that more often."

"I did, Dad." Hank said. "And I got detention."

"Well, that's not real life. That's middle school. In real life you've got to look out for yourself because nobody is going to do it for you. You'll never get anywhere in this world unless you're assertive. You've got to be more assertive."

Hank knew he wasn't talking about the fight anymore or even about school. He meant basketball. He thought Hank was too unassertive. He felt Hank would be playing more if he demanded more time, the way the other kids did. The way the other kids' fathers did.

And frankly, Hank might *earn* more playing time if he were more assertive. If he played harder.

At least, that's what his father thought.

Hank knew he already *was* playing as hard as he could.

"Are you in here for fighting?" Mrs. Cooperman said. She took out a couple of plastic containers and placed them on top of her desk.

Hank nodded.

"I can see that. You look like some kind of tough guy. So where's your friend? He's supposed to be here, too."

They both looked at the clock as the little hand clicked into place and just as it did, Jeremy walked in.

"Hope you two brought a snack," Mrs. Cooperman said.

"But I thought we weren't allowed to eat in here," Hank said.

Mrs. Cooperman took a big forkful of her salad. "Well," she said. "That's true. But I don't like to eat alone so you better bring something for tomorrow." Mrs. Cooperman looked down at the computer sheet in front of her. "And we have another day together, so bring cookies if you can. I like cookies."

Anabel

Anabel was late for the fourth day in a row.

She missed the bus and her dad had to drive her to school. He wasn't getting this Mr. Mom thing very well. He was late. By the time he pulled into the drop-off line, all the other cars were gone. The doors were shut. Not a good sign.

"I'm sorry, Anabel, but those are the rules. Three unexcused tardies and you get detention."

Anabel stood at the counter in the main office. She needed a late pass, and she got detention instead. If it helped any, the attendance secretary looked really sorry as she wrote out the slip. Really, she did.

"What period do you have lunch?" the secretary asked.

"Fifth, but I'm staying in for my science project," Anabel said.

"How about fourth? What do you have fourth?"

"English."

The secretary was shaking her head. "Well, next week is sixth-grade testing. I'm sorry, Anabel, you'll have to stay after for detention. Tomorrow. I'll send a note home. Oh, now it's okay. Don't get upset. It's not that bad. Anabel, I'll explain it to your mother. Don't worry."

Anabel didn't know who to feel worse for, herself or the secretary. The secretary looked like *she* was going to cry.

"It's okay," Anabel whispered.

"I'll call your mother. I'll tell her it's no big deal. It's just one of those silly school rules."

"Sure," Anabel said. She imagined the answering machine at home picking up the call. It got nestled in between a call about AAU tryouts and team photo day; nobody would even hear it.

TRAP

The next move was a clandestine masterpiece. Coach Vince quit and Tyler Bischoff's dad quietly took over the team. There was a lot of speculation as to why Coach Vince actually left, especially after he had brought the team to its one and only victory.

Most parents agreed it was the parents. Every parent other than themselves, of course.

There was a rumor going around that right after the game, Coach Vince got no less than nine phone calls at home. The phone calls ranged from, "My kid didn't play enough" to "What are your qualifications for coaching?" to "Maybe we could get together at my club and play a little golf in the spring," and that

Coach Vince could see the writing on the wall. And he just quit. He told the boys at the last practice that he had too many obligations with work and his new home, but he looked genuinely upset. The boys were, too. They liked Coach Vince.

"Who's going to be our new coach?" Matt King asked.

"I don't know, Matt. Mr. Bischoff will be talking to you now. Maybe he has a better idea about that."

Tyler's dad was standing in the gym, leaning against the wall under the hoop. When he heard his name he pushed off with his back and stepped forward to "say a few words."

He spoke for over thirty-five minutes, while the boys sat cross-legged on the floor. He talked about getting through these minor bumps in the road. He talked about the future of the team. About having a winning attitude. About working hard and how most of the learning is done at practice. Playing during a game was only a small part of it all.

Then he talked about *his* school days, playing basketball and baseball in high school and then, yes, in college. He told them how he was on his all-state basketball team and that *he* came from a much bigger town. And it had a much more "diverse" population than North Bridge, he added. Only a few kids knew what he meant by that. Mr. Bischoff went on to say that he was looking forward to a positive season from here on in.

"So who's going to be our new coach?" Matt King asked again.

"Are you really that dumb?" Michael Morrisey said out loud.

Then Harrison Neeley said his butt hurt from sitting on the floor for so long, and Hank Adler said he had to go to the bathroom.

It was past time to go anyway.

DETENTION

"What are *you* doing in here?"

Nathan was not surprised to see Hank and Jeremy in detention (he had heard about the fight in the cafeteria, of course), but they were apparently surprised to see him.

"Is this detention?" Nathan asked.

"Yeah, and what are you doing here?" Jeremy asked again.

"It doesn't look like detention."

"Well, it is," Hank Adler said.

"So what's she doing here?" Nathan pointed to Anabel Morrisey. There was no way she'd be in detention.

"I was late. What are *you* doing here?" Anabel

asked. She was sitting at a long table reading a book and munching chips out of a huge bag. It didn't look like detention.

"Where's the teacher?" Nathan asked. He was still standing in the doorway.

"What's the matter with you?" Jeremy said. He threw a balled-up piece of paper at Nathan.

"It's Mrs. Cooperman, and I don't think she likes having detention duty very much," Hank explained. "She kind of wanders in and out."

"Oh." Nathan stepped into the room.

"So?" Jeremy asked. "Whatcha do?"

Nathan hesitated. His reason for getting detention was going to sound so stupid and he knew it. For a second he considered saying that he had cursed at a teacher or pushed or something good like that, but nobody was going to believe him. Besides, lying all the time to his parents was beginning to eat away at his stomach lining. Nathan had been trying to figure out how to get a prescription for the "little purple pill." He was sure he had an ulcer.

"I didn't get my test signed," Nathan said.

"You failed a test?" Anabel said. "You never get anything below a ninety-five."

"I got an eighty-three," Nathan said. Might as well tell the whole truth.

"An eighty-three!" Hank yelled. "You were afraid

to tell your parents you got an eighty-three?"

"Get out of here," Jeremy yelled, too.

"Get out of here," Anabel yelled.

They all started throwing wadded-up pieces of paper at Nathan. He covered his head and ducked. The last ball of paper hit Mrs. Cooperman right in the nose, only it wasn't Mrs. Cooperman, it was Mr. Bernardino.

They all got another day of detention.

And a warning.

One more infraction (*infraction*, that was really the word Mr. Bernardino used), and they would be suspended from the travel basketball team.

"But I'm not on the team," Anabel spoke up.

"And you won't be, Miss Morrisey!" Mr. Bernardino shot back. "Take my word for it."

It took everything they had to keep from laughing until Mr. Bernardino had left, slamming the door behind him. And then there was no stopping them.

Jeremy

The first change Mr. Bischoff made was his starting lineup. He had some reason for the change. Something that had to do with using his big guys more and a different offense than the coaches before him had used.

The new starting lineup was now Michael Morrisey, Hank Adler, Julian Rizzoto, Matt King, and Tyler Bischoff.

Camden Tomasello and Harrison Neeley had the flu, and Sam Bernegger was away. That left five kids to practice. Perfect. Five on five.

"I've got some new plays to show everyone," Mr. Bischoff said. He was holding the dry-erase board with a diagram of the court. "We are going to learn some real basketball. Today we are going to focus on offense."

All the boys were pretty quiet. Why wasn't Jeremy starting? He was so clearly one of the best, if not *the* best player on the team.

But no one said anything.

Mr. Bischoff ran the practice hard. He kept the "starting" five together the whole time and concentrated on teaching them the offensive plays. He used the other five to run the defense.

Defense only.

Jeremy figured out what was going on before anyone else. It was so obvious. It was like everything else in life. It wasn't worth saying anything. It's always the same.

But he didn't care. Until somebody else noticed.

"This is a load of crap," Hank whispered to

Jeremy. They were both getting a drink in the hall. They were allowed one break.

"What?"

"Bischoff just wants his kid to make all the points. All the plays are to Tyler. Wanna Gatorade? I got extra."

When Hank opened his gym bag, Jeremy saw two Gatorades and a bottle of Aquafina inside.

Jeremy shrugged. "Okay." He took a Gatorade.

"I mean, why do you think he's not starting you. You're the best kid on the team. It's just stupid."

From inside the gym Mr. Bischoff blew the whistle.

"My dad hates Mr. Bischoff," Hank went on.

"Your dad?" Jeremy said. He wiped the water from his chin.

Hank started back into the gym. "Yeah, my dad's going to go crazy when he sees this. Except he thinks I should be starting, so I guess maybe he'll be happy. It's so messed up."

Jeremy thought for a minute what his own dad might have thought of all this. Would he be mad, like these other dads would? Ranting on about how his son wasn't getting enough playing time? That his son deserved more. Asking for a fair chance. Demanding one?

"C'mon," Hank said. He started back to the gym.

"We gotta go back."

What for?

Jeremy stood a minute in the empty hall. Hank was already inside. The door was closing behind him. As Jeremy yanked on the heavy door, he had a weird feeling, a sense, and he thought he saw him again.

His father.

Disappearing around the lockers.

You couldn't be sure. It happened so quickly. Like a mirage.

Something you see because you want it so badly.

Jeremy

It wasn't official. Of course, it wasn't official, but the two practice teams already had nicknames. The Starters and the Benchers. The chosen five and the other boys who were destined to sit on the bench the whole game. And Jeremy. The two teams scrimmaged against each other at the end of each practice.

"What the hell are you doing, Binder?"

Jeremy didn't stop. He had stolen the ball from Michael and tore off down court for a layup. The other boys just stood where they had been placed by Mr. Bischoff.

"Binder!" Mr. Bischoff screamed again. "You do

what I tell you and when I tell you to do it. Understand?"

It was the third time in a row Jeremy had stolen the ball from the point guard, who just happened to be the coach's son, Tyler. Jeremy made a layup each time. The "starting" team couldn't even get the ball downcourt.

"We are trying to run a play, goddamn it!" Bischoff screamed some more. "Once more and you're sitting the whole next game. Now set it up. Tyler, take the point."

The boys got into position and Tyler starting dribbling down. He passed half-court but that was about it. Jeremy darted out on the first pass, reached with his hand, and stole the ball. There was something infectious about his energy. The rest of his team followed. Jeremy called out. He passed to Julian, who threw the ball back to Jeremy. Jeremy looked up. Nathan (also a bencher) was standing right under the hoop. He threw a hard bounce pass that by some luck Nathan happened to catch.

"Put it up," Jeremy called out.

Nathan turned and shot. He was completely off balance and barely facing the hoop. The ball rolled around the rim three times and then dropped in. It was his first basket all year.

"You're out of this practice, Binder. Get dressed!"

Mr. Bischoff was puffed out like his head was a tied-off balloon. His face was red and beads of sweat formed a little line across his forehead.

Jeremy didn't care. He didn't need this garbage. He was glad he got kicked out.

It would just make it easier to leave, that's all.

Hank

"So you're a starter," Hank's dad said. He tried to put his arm around Hank as they walked out into the parking lot after practice.

Hank stepped away.

"Yeah, I guess."

Yeah. He was a starter. It felt good. Of course, they hadn't played a real game yet, but it felt good. Didn't it?

It felt great.

Tyler's dad was a tough coach. He was mean, actually, but he seemed to know basketball. He taught them some stuff, some plays. He finally got Matt King to set a pick in the right place. He got Michael Morrisey to dribble with his head up. He told Hank to keep his elbows in when he was shooting.

But then there was Jeremy. Mr. Bischoff hated

Jeremy, and there just wasn't any reason for it. Except maybe that Jeremy was kind of fresh. He didn't talk back exactly, but he *held* something back. He didn't smile. He didn't agree with everything.

And Jeremy was good. He was really good. He was definitely better than Mr. Bischoff's son, Tyler, and they played the same position. Jeremy should definitely be starting. Certainly before Hank.

So who was going to complain? Who was going to say anything? Hank could just hear it now.

Oh, yeah, Adler? So you think your friend Jeremy should be starting. Well, that's fine. I guess you can just sit your ass right down on the bench next to him then. For the rest of the season.

"I knew you'd make your way to the top. It was just a matter of time. It takes a while for a coach to see which kids should be playing where. That's reasonable," Hank's father was saying. They were driving home.

"Mr. Bischoff's just been the coach for a week, Dad. What could he know?"

"He's watched you boys for years. He's seen you play soccer and baseball. An athlete is an athlete. He can see that."

"I thought you hated Mr. Bischoff. I thought you said he favored his own kid and he'd do anything to get Tyler every advantage."

"I never said I *hated* him, Hank."

"Yes, you did. Worse."

"No, I didn't. I would never say *hate*. I might not agree with his style. Hey, so when's your next game?" Hank's father changed the subject.

"Not for a couple of weeks. We have midwinter break, remember? That's why Sam Bernegger's away. They left early to go to St. Bart's."

"Is there practice?"

"Yeah, Mr. Bischoff said he'd try to get us the YMCA while school's closed."

"Well, good. That gives us some time to work on skills. Before your first game."

Us?

Hank looked at his dad. He was so happy about this. He was happier than Hank. And confident. How could he be so confident? Hank wasn't.

Something was so not right in this universe.

Nathan

"I need help." Nathan just came out and said it.

He had been watching Jeremy at recess. Even though it was cold, Jeremy was out on the blacktop shooting hoops. He played out there every day, regardless of the weather. Most days Hank Adler played with him, but today Jeremy was alone and

Nathan took the opportunity.

"Mr. Bischoff will help you," Jeremy answered. He took a jump shot and grabbed his own rebound. He kept dribbling around while Nathan was trying to talk to him.

"Yeah, right," Nathan said.

Jeremy stopped. "Okay. But so what? He's a jerk. Who cares about Bischoff?"

Jeremy picked up his dribble again. Then he turned and passed the ball to Nathan.

"I don't care about Mr. Bischoff," Nathan said. He held the basketball as if protecting his stomach. "I've got bigger problems. So will you help me or not?" Nathan bounced the ball a few times and positioned himself to shot.

"Bend your knees," Jeremy said.

Nathan figured that was a yes.

"And hold the ball like this," Jeremy said. "Two hands."

Nathan bent his knees and held the ball in two hands. He threw the ball up at the net. And missed.

"I suck," Nathan said.

"No you don't," Jeremy said. He stopped the ball with his foot before it rolled away. He dribbled back a few steps and shot again. *Swish.* Nathan got the ball and held onto it. He squared up, under the hoop.

"No wait," Jeremy said. "Two hands. And make

your shooting arm like a perfect L. So if you take your left hand away, the ball shouldn't fall."

Nathan followed the directions. He made his shooting arm like an L.

"Face your toes to the basket," Jeremy said.

Nathan shifted his feet.

"Aim for the center of the basket and shoot at the top of your jump."

Nathan bent his knees, jumped, shot—

And missed again.

"Yes I do," Nathan said.

Jeremy started to say something then he stopped.

"I really suck."

"Okay, so what if you do?" Jeremy said finally.

So what?

"It's basketball. It's just a game. Nobody here is going to be playing after high school. They'll be lucky if they *get* to play in high school. You should see kids that are really good."

"You're really good," Nathan said.

It was just something about the way Jeremy handled the ball. The way he saw the court and knew where to pass and where to stand, how to move.

Jeremy kept dribbling and shooting. "So, what's your story, Nat?" he said finally.

Which story might that be? The story about the uncle who almost played professional basketball but didn't seem to pass on any of those basketball genes. The story about his father who says basketball is a waste of time but expects his son to be really good at it. Which story?

"My father said he's going to come to our next game. And he's going to find out I've been lying," Nathan said. He wrapped his arms around the ball and held it to his chest.

"Lying about what?"

"I'd tell him things I did that I really didn't do. I just took what someone else did and I said it was me." Nathan starting dribbling.

"Like what? What did you tell him?" Jeremy asked. He didn't ask for the ball. He just listened.

Nathan dropped the ball to the ground and bounced it twice. He faced the basket, raised his arms, elbow in, and let go. The ball rolled unsteadily around the metal rim.

"I told him I was you," Nathan said. They both watched as the basketball missed the net and dropped off into the grass.

Anabel

For the seven years Anabel had been in public school, she had never gotten detention, and now she had two in as many days. Something was wrong with this picture. Besides, she was in detention with her brother's basketball friends. Some of the boys she saw every practice and all weekend long, sweating and running all over the place.

It was disgusting.

Although, Jeremy was kind of cute. And Hank had a nice smile. Nathan was really smart and kind of cute, but boy, he really couldn't play basketball.

The detention teacher wasn't even in the room. She never was. She just took attendance and walked out. There were only the four of them, sitting at four different desks, all spread across the room. Staring out the window. It was the end of December. Light enough out and warm somedays that you could almost remember spring. There had been a lot of early snow, and it still covered most of the ground.

"I'm outta here," Jeremy said suddenly.

"What?" Hank said.

Jeremy stood up. "Let's go. Why are we sitting? Let's just go."

"Where?" Nathan asked.

Anabel just watched. She knew no one was talking to her anyway. She had a vision of Mrs. Cooperman walking in and seeing only Anabel sitting nicely at her desk with her hands folded. She was always the good one.

"To the gym. There's no one there now. Let's just go," Jeremy said.

Hank stood up right away.

"We can't," Nathan said. "We're in detention."

"So?" Hank said. "Don't be a—" He stopped when he saw Anabel.

"Come on," Jeremy said. "We can work on your shot."

That should work.

It did. Nathan stood up. He looked around as if someone was watching and then he followed behind Jeremy and Hank.

Anabel looked out the window again. The snow was melting in little patches all over, with bits of soaking wet, smushed-down, yellowy grass poking through. There was something really lonely about that.

Anabel's mother was in Florida that week. She had called the house just that morning before school.

"It's warm and sunny down here," Anabel's mother sang out from the speaker phone. Everyone was rushing around trying to get ready for work and the school bus. Anabel was determined not to miss it again.

"So stay there," her dad said. He said it sort of under his breath, like maybe he forgot she was on speaker, or maybe he didn't realize how loud he had said it, or maybe he meant it.

Anabel and Michael stopped what they were doing and looked at each other, but they didn't say anything. It was an awful morning. Their dad picked up the receiver and Anabel and Michael knew their parents were fighting. She ran out to the bus without saying good-bye, and somehow now she was sitting here, all alone in detention.

"Are you coming or what?" It was Jeremy. He had popped his head back into the classroom.

"What?" Anabel turned from the window.

"Come on," Jeremy said. His hand was holding onto the door frame and half his body was still out in the hall, like a giant vacuum was pulling him.

"Where?"

God, wasn't that dumb?

Jeremy let go of the door frame, but he stood there waiting. "Just come on already."

Anabel looked out the window one more second at the withering, pathetic, yellow grass. And she decided to go.

COURTSIDE

"**I**'m not playing two-on-two with a girl," Hank was saying.

Nathan was sitting on the ball. From time to time he'd look toward the door to see if anyone was coming.

"So we'll play H-O-R-S-E or Around the World," Jeremy offered. "Nathan can work on his shot. You know, bend his knees."

"Around the World. Fine with me," Anabel said. She stood on the left side of the basket and held out her hands for the ball. Nathan stood up and passed it to her.

"I'm second," Hank got ready to take Anabel's place when she missed. But she didn't. And she didn't miss the next shot or the next or the one after that. The boys were silent.

"Where did you learn to shoot like that," Jeremy said finally.

"I spent my whole life in a gym," Anabel answered. "I've been playing basketball with my brother in the driveway since I could walk. What do you think?"

"So why don't you play?" Hank asked her.

"I just hate basketball." Anabel stepped over to the next position and shot again.

"I wish I could hate basketball like that," Nathan said, watching Anabel's shot slip through the net without a sound.

Anabel made the foul shot, but missed on her fifth shot from the far right-hand corner outside the three-point line. She passed the ball to Hank. "Your turn."

Hank made his first two shots and missed the third. Jeremy did the same and passed the ball to Nathan.

"I don't want to play." Nathan looked around at Anabel and Hank. He looked at Jeremy and then down at the ground.

"C'mon, Nathan. Play," Hank said.

Nathan didn't move.

Anabel suddenly wanted to play really badly. "Yeah, Nathan. It's my turn next. Shoot."

And then something changed. The mood. They could just feel it. Nathan held the ball as if it gave him courage.

"I've got to tell my dad the truth," he said finally.

"What truth?" Anabel asked. And he told them.

Mrs. Cooperman never came looking for them. The basketball rolled to the other end of the gym and stayed there quietly, the whole period, just listening. First they just started talking about Nathan and how much better he'd feel when he came clean about the whole thing. It was actually a pretty funny story, but none of them laughed. Then they started talking about Mr. Bischoff and how mean he was. And how mean he really was to Jeremy and what had happened in practice. And how unfair it was. It was all so unfair.

And then Jeremy told them a little bit about how he came to live with his grandmother. About his father. About Lannie.

"But I'm not staying," Jeremy said. "I'm leaving right after our next game. I'm taking my grandmother's car. At halftime."

They were all sitting on the floor by the blue foam wrapped around the basketball pole. It was obvious from the way he spoke, from the way he sounded, that Jeremy had been planning this for a while. He was certain.

"I'm going Saturday," Jeremy told them.

Anabel, Hank, and Nathan were quiet.

"You can't tell anyone," Jeremy said suddenly. "You have to promise." He stuck out his hand. It seemed so strange. Not real and yet too real. No one could move.

Hank was the first to agree. He slowly reached out his hand.

"No wait," Jeremy said jumping up. "We need a special handshake."

That was enough to break up the tension.

"Yeah, a special handshake." Nathan got to his feet. Anabel and Hank stood and huddled in.

They started various moves on each other, ranging from a respectable shake with a pull and a finger waggle with a head tap to a fist bang, shake into a finger draw, ending with a chest bang. What they ended up with was an elaborate handshake, with a bang, a wiggle, a thumb-touching thing, and a firm grip ending.

No one was allowed to talk about what Jeremy was planning.

Promise.

Jeremy agreed he would come back and visit.

Promise.

Nathan was going to tell his dad the truth before the next game.

Promise.

Anabel said she would try out for the girls' basketball team next year.

Promise.

"So what are you promising?" Jeremy asked Hank. It took a few seconds to complete each handshake, three times for all four of them. The bell had already rung. It was time to go.

"I don't know yet," Hank said. "But something. I promise."

Nathan

The night before the game—the game his father said he was going to come to—Nathan created this elaborate fantasy in his mind. It had to do with his uncle. Even though Nathan had never meet his uncle, he had a picture of what he'd look like. Kind of scruffy, but tall and muscular. Of course, you couldn't tell because his clothes would be baggy and not very nice. Short hair. Tall, naturally. Very tall. And handsome, in that broken, hard-luck sort of way.

He'd show up at the game because he heard that his nephew was playing basketball, and he'd drive four hours to tell him to give it up. Basketball ruins your life. So naturally, but regretfully, Nathan would have to step down from the team and not play. He'd have to listen to the advice of his uncle. His uncle was a professional, after all. And he knew what he was talking about.

Or better, the other team would show up. They'd come running into the gym all in a row, and jogging behind them would be their coach. And wait. Oh, no. Ohmigod, what a coincidence. Nathan's father would stagger down off the bleachers. He would be without words (wouldn't that be nice) because the coach of the other team was his brother.

It was incredible. Amazing. After all these years.

Of course, they would all be so overcome with emotion no one could play. The game would be called off. Okay, so maybe that wouldn't happen.

It would never happen.

Besides, Nathan had already made a promise. He shook on it. He would tell his dad everything.

Right now.

Or maybe tomorrow.

Jeremy

Jeremy packed what he thought he would want to have with him for the rest of his life and went to bed. He had packed his clothes. His toothbrush. His sneakers. His CD player and his CDs. His Old

Spice scented deodorant/antiperspirant. He needed that.

No books. All of his money and a little of his grandmother's. He thought she would want him to have it.

He knew she would.

Actually, he hadn't given much thought to what his grandmother would think of his running away. He didn't want to think about that. It was hard enough trying to convince himself he was doing the right thing. Looking for the place where he belonged. It was the logical move. And now that he had told everyone, he had to do it.

When he was trying to shut the zipper and the clasp of his duffel bag, the one he had showed up here with, it wouldn't shut. Something hard was sticking out sideways, and the zipper teeth wouldn't come together. Jeremy opened his bag back up and took out the frame, his father's high-school graduation diploma. There was something that made him want it. He wasn't sure what it was, but he wanted it.

It was something that had more to do with the frame than the diploma itself. It had something to do with being young and having someone frame your diploma. He wanted it. He took out all the clothing and shoved the frame to the very bottom. When all the clothes were stuffed on top, the whole thing closed and zipped up.

He was ready. He'd go to sleep that night. The game was Saturday. Tomorrow. He'd leave at half-time. This was going to be his last night in North Bridge. All he had to do was fall asleep and it would be tomorrow. Then his grandmother's voice came up the stairs.

"Jeremy, don't forget to brush your teeth."

"Yeah, okay," Jeremy shouted back down.

He slipped his feet out of his covers.

It was so stupid. He didn't have to brush his teeth. He didn't have to do anything. He flipped on the light. There was an electric razor on the side of the sink. Brand new. It was opened and plugged in, but the wrapper and the instructions were right next to it.

There was no one else in the house. This was for him. Jeremy looked closer in the mirror. Was he supposed to shave?

He looked even closer.

There was a line of fine dark hair just over his lip that did give him that never-clean face. And it had gotten darker and longer just recently. Like it had happened so slowly that one day it was just there. A little mustache.

Was his grandmother telling him he should shave?

Kids in school had teased him about it. Some of the older kids. Some of the girls. It didn't make him uncomfortable, exactly, but sort of. Like in gym, Jeremy didn't like to change. Most of the other boys barely had hair on their legs. A little fuzz, but not like his. Jeremy wore sweatpants whenever he could.

He picked up the razor. It was kind of cool. There was a little red light, an energy indicator. Cool.

It must have been an expensive razor. Jeremy turned it on, and when it began to buzz he flipped it off again. He stood there looking into the mirror and tried to remember the last time he saw his father shaving.

This was really an expensive razor. It was self cleaning.

Was he supposed to shave under his nose? Or all around? Under his chin? He was trying to remember. Jeremy stretched his top lip over his teeth and turned the razor on again.

It stung a little. Not when he was shaving but after he was done. Like chapped lips but not on his lips, but just for a little while. And look, the dark hair was gone.

He did look better.

Jeremy looked at himself in the mirror for a long time. It was funny, you could stare at one little part of your face for so long it starts to look like it doesn't belong. Like your nose. You could look at just your nose until it doesn't look familiar to you at all. Not one bit. But you know it's *your* nose. The same nose you had yesterday and the day before. Maybe you aren't supposed to look at your face like that.

Maybe you have to look at the whole thing.

Who am I?

Where do I belong?

Jeremy knew why he had to go.

He just wasn't sure he really wanted to anymore.

FULL-COURT PRESS

North Bridge was expected to lose tomorrow's game. Hollis was a very similar town. The two schools were only a few miles apart. The towns bordered each other. If you were an outsider, you'd just think it was a spillover of the same white, affluent, spoiled kids from one town into the other and back again. If you were an outsider.

Hollis was bigger. They had a movie theater and a Starbucks and a Super Stop & Shop. They had a swimming pool in their high school and Astroturf on their football field. And every year they kicked North Bridge's butt in almost every sport—skiing, tennis, golf, baseball, football, lacrosse, and swimming. But basketball was always a toss-up.

Neither town seemed to have a clear advantage. Neither town seemed to grow any seven-foot-six Yao Ming types.

If North Bridge had ridiculously fancy sixth-grade travel team uniforms, Hollis was sure to have fancier. If the North Bridge eighth-grade travel team all went to Allan Houston's sleepaway camp in Westchester, New York, together, Hollis's team went to Chicago, to the Michael Jordan sleepaway basketball camp. And if the following year, North Bridge hired an ex-professional basketball coach from Hartford, Hollis got one from New York City. And paid his expenses.

It was a typical, suburban, elitist sports rivalry.

Let the better team buy the win.

Anabel

Anabel found herself making up all these crazy scenarios while she was getting ready for bed. Michael had been sent to bed half an hour ago. He didn't play well unless he had nine hours minimum.

While she was brushing her teeth, Anabel thought about what would happen if somehow—and she couldn't figure out exactly how this would happen—but what if somehow, tomorrow, there were only four kids left who could play?

The referee blows his whistle and calls North Bridge out onto the court. The coach is looking frantic.

"We'll have to play with four," he says to the boys in the huddle.

Jeremy looks up at the scoreboard. Of course, North Bridge is losing by two points, and there are only five minutes left in the game. No, three. Make that three minutes.

(Jeremy *is* playing, of course, because Mr. Bischoff gets the flu and the other dad who takes over isn't crazy enough to bench the best player for the most important game of the season.)

"We can't play with four players." That's Michael talking. "We'll get killed."

The other boys all nod their hanging heads.

"We have to. We don't have a choice," the coach tells them.

The referee is getting impatient.

"Wait," Jeremy Binder says suddenly. "I have an idea."

The coach looks like he is listening. The other team is already on the court.

"What about Anabel?" Jeremy says.

"Anabel?" Michael says. "You mean my *sister*?"

"Who?" the coach asks.

"Trust me," Jeremy says. He looks over to

Michael, who realizes this might not be such a bad idea.

"But she's not on the roster," the coach says. "We'll get a technical if we put out a player who's not on the list."

They look around at one another. Then suddenly Jeremy . . . No, it's Michael. Suddenly Michael says, "She can take my place. Nobody will know. It only says Morrisey on the roster. Nobody will know."

At this point Anabel stopped brushing her teeth and looked right into the mirror.

"You idiot, that makes four players again," she said out loud.

Hank

"I washed your uniform for tomorrow's game."

When Hank didn't respond to that, his mother said, "It's on your bed."

Hank was sitting in his room at his desk. His mother was outside his door, wishing she were inside. Wishing, Hank was sure, that he would invite her in and talk about tomorrow's game.

"Do you see it?" Her voice came through pretty loud, like she had her mouth right up to the door frame.

Hank took a deep breath. He was staring at his computer screen.

"Yeah," he answered. Hank had his away-message on the screen—TOO MUCH HOMEWORK—but a lot of his friends were still trying to IM him. He recognized Nathan's screen name, Natman002.

But he didn't respond. He waited until he heard his mother's footsteps move away from his door and then he signed off at 9:32 P.M. It was the night before the game. The big game. He was a starter.

Hank shut down his computer and got ready for bed, and then he just lay there.

Hank had read somewhere that it is supposed to take at least fifteen minutes to fall asleep and if you fall asleep faster than that, it means you are too tired and you aren't getting enough sleep. An hour and a half had gone by already. Hank would almost fall asleep, but then he started thinking all over again. He was exhausted but wide awake. So much for that theory.

Hank didn't want Jeremy to leave, but he could understand. At least, he thought he could understand. He could understand feeling like you just have to run. Get out. Get away. In a way, Jeremy was lucky. At least he had somewhere to go.

Didn't he?

When Hank was little he used to watch the

ballgames with his dad—baseball, football, basketball. Even hockey. Sometimes tennis. Golf.

There would always come a play, a second, a moment when the game was on the line. When everything could go one way or it could go another, and it always came down to one guy.

And if he made it, if that one guy came through and made the play, got the rebound, blocked the shot, scored the goal, threw the pass, whatever it was, if he *did* it, everyone would be cheering and shouting. Everyone would love him. They'd win. They'd score. They'd make the play-offs or the World Series or the Superbowl.

But if that one guy *didn't*, Hank's father, sitting in his living room watching the ballgame with his son, would always say the same thing.

"He coulda been a hero."

Anabel

The seating arrangement had changed, Anabel noticed. She noticed it right away. It was almost like the new starting five parents had moved to sit together, right in front. The parents of kids who played very little, but whose parents thought they should play more, stayed together and a few rows back. And again, those whose parents were furious sat way in the back, very close together so they could commiserate. Only Camden Tomasello's mom and dad, who were always happy no matter what, didn't seem to notice the hierarchy of seat placement and just sat anywhere.

Matt's dad was sitting pretty high up and off to the side, but Anabel was a few steps higher and could see the stopwatch hidden in his hand. Wyatt's dad was sitting right next to Matt's dad, preparing to time the amount of minutes their kids got to play compared to . . . oh . . . let's say . . . Tyler Bischoff. Anabel was only surprised other fathers hadn't thought of that before. Clicking away the seconds, documenting the ultimate injustice.

Perfect.

And as always, Jeremy's grandmother made her way up the bleachers to sit next to Anabel.

"Well, I had a hard time finding this place. I turned left at the stop sign instead of right," she said. She let out a huff of air as she sat.

Anabel felt guilty immediately. His grandmother would want to know, Anabel thought. She would want to know how Jeremy felt. What he was thinking. What he was planning. All parents, probably grandparents, too, always wanted to know what their kids were thinking. Even when they didn't care, when they weren't going to do anything to change anything or fix anything, they still wanted to know.

But even if she hadn't made that promise (but she had), there was a very strong wall between the world of grown-ups and the world of kids. Nancy Binder was definitely a grown-up.

"He seemed so distant this morning," Jeremy's grandmother went on, almost to herself. "Not that he's been exactly open to me. Not since he's gotten here. Not since ever, really. . . but I'm not going to give up. That's what they say, isn't it? Keep trying because that way they know you care. Isn't that what they say?"

There was such sadness in those words. Anabel didn't answer. She couldn't. Instead, she looked down at the court. The boys were warming up, looping around in semicircles, dribbling and shooting and passing the ball around like a ritual dance.

START TIME

"So did you tell your dad?" Hank asked Nathan.
Jeremy sat next to him waiting for the answer.

Nathan nodded his head and then he said, "Well, not exactly."

Hank and Jeremy waited for the rest.

"I tried. I mean, I wanted to. But well, then I couldn't."

The game was going to start any minute. They were all on the bench together, down at the far end, in a row. One two three.

"You think he'll notice?" Nathan asked. "That I'm not playing."

Jeremy looked up into the bleachers where Nathan's parents and baby sister were sitting.

"Well, he has a camera," Jeremy said.

"A what? He really brought that camera?" Nathan slid his feet out and slouched down as much as he could.

Hank turned to look. "Yeah, he did."

"With the telephoto lens?" Nathan asked.

"Looks like it," Jeremy said.

"Oh, God."

"Hey, look on the bright side," Jeremy said to Nathan.

"What's that?"

"You can keep me company on the bench." Jeremy laughed.

"That's not funny," Hank said. "It sucks. It's not fair."

"So are you really going to leave?" Nathan asked Jeremy in a whisper.

Jeremy jingled something metal inside his pocket as an answer. "The extra car keys," he said.

Hank and Nathan were quiet.

All three of them stared straight ahead at the empty court. There was something wrong with the clock. The two refs and the two coaches were trying to get it sorted out. Random numbers kept flashing on the board, different scores and different times. Every couple of seconds the time-out buzzer would sound, and everyone would cover their ears.

"It's not right," Hank said to Jeremy. "You should be playing. It's not fair."

"Everything's like that," Jeremy said. "Why should this be any different?"

"Because it should be," Nathan answered.

"Yeah, it should be," Hank said. " Something's got to be fair, doesn't it? Shouldn't it?"

Jeremy shrugged. "Well, it isn't. Nothing is."

Three pairs of bony knees stuck out from blue shorts, banging together nervously, as the assistant coach of the other team walked by, lugging a mesh bag full of basketballs over his shoulder.

"They look big," Hank said.

The three boys turned to the Hollis bench. They were big. Not only did they have matching uniforms with their last names on the back, they had warm-ups and water bottles with their school insignia. Their matching gym bags were lined up against the wall. The Hollis players were sitting on their bench, waiting. And they *were* big.

"I think we need to do some birth certificate checks," Jeremy said. "I think that kid, number fifteen, is growing a beard."

"Number forty-five has been in sixth grade for three years," Hank said.

"I think that kid has been buying growth hormones off the Internet," Nathan added.

Suddenly the buzzer blasted. Everyone startled.

"We almost have it fixed, folks. Thanks for your patience," Mr. Bischoff called out to the crowd. He stood in the center of the floor.

"If I were a good friend, I'd do something," Hank said, watching him.

"About what?" Jeremy asked.

"I don't know. I'd say something. It's not fair. It just sucks. Mr. Bischoff just wants Tyler to play. He wants Tyler to be the best. And he's not. Not even close."

Jeremy answered Hank, "Forget it. It has nothing to do with you. With being a friend or not."

The buzzer screamed out again, and this time it didn't stop. Five seconds later it cleared and was silent. All the lights on the board went out and on again, and then off. It was fixed.

The referees walked out onto the court and got ready. Mr. Bischoff called the team into a huddle. The boys stood up. Michael, Julian, Matt, Harrison, Camden, and Sam. Joey, Scott, and Tyler. Hank and Jeremy and Nathan. Mr. Bischoff read off the names of the starting five. No surprise.

"You're wrong," Hank said before he went out.

"Wrong about what?" Nathan asked.

"Not you," Hank said.

The other team was standing, ready for the jump. The referee had the ball held up in the air and a whistle dangling from his lips.

"It *is* about being a friend," Hank said, more to himself than anyone in particular, as he walked out onto the court.

THIRTY-SECOND
TIME-OUT

Tyler Bischoff's dad, who had been an only semisane, type A personality, a get-up-wipe-the-blood-off-your-face-and-play kind of coach in practice, suddenly changed when the game started.

He got worse.

Mr. Bischoff scared some of the players. North Bridge was already losing by five points in the first five minutes. Mr. Bischoff's face had grown a deeper shade of red for every point. He called a time-out. A full-minute time-out.

"Hank, what the hell are you doing out there? That number twelve is getting by you every time. I've never seen you play worse! What the hell are you doing?"

The boys were standing in a circle around Mr. Bischoff. Even the boys sitting on the bench were expected to get up and huddle around. Mr. Bischoff was in the center, kneeling down with his clipboard on his bent leg.

"You guys are playing like shit." His voice was held inside the thick circle of sweaty bodies. "They are beating us on the boards. Can you get one god-damn rebound, Matt. And Hank, what the hell are you doing out there! If twelve gets by you one more time, you're out. Do you hear me? I'll pull you right out of there!"

Hank didn't respond because that was exactly what he hoped would happen.

It was his promise.

Jeremy

Hank was stinking up the place big-time. He had lost the ball five times already. He had let that little guard on the other team get right by him. The kid was faking left. Every time. Hank must see that. Bischoff had just chewed him out real bad. He was furious with Hank and would pull him, Jeremy was sure.

"One two three North Bridge!"

Everyone repeated the shout. "North Bridge. Let's win!"

Jeremy tried to tell Hank. Get his attention. *Go right. He's faking. He can't even dribble with his left hand.* But Hank turned his head away quickly and ran out onto the court. And that's when Jeremy figured it out.

Hank was doing it on purpose.

Jeremy forced himself to turn and look into the bleachers. Normally he never did that. He never wanted to see all the other parents. Hank's dad was there. He had a pained look on his face. Hank was doing a really good job of looking good at playing bad. It must have been killing his father.

Hollis was bringing the ball down fast. Hank was waiting just at the half-court line. He was leaning down, knees bent. He looked ready. He had his eyes on the ball as it got closer and closer.

The kid did it again. He faked left with that same stupid expression on his face. He *wasn't* going to go left. He *couldn't*. It was the most obvious thing in the world, and Hank went for it just as Jeremy predicted. But it took Jeremy another second or two to figure out why. Why would Hank deliberately get pulled from the game?

Suddenly it was so obvious. Hank was playing like shit so that the coach would pull him. And with Wyatt out sick, there'd only be one guard left.

Jeremy.

He was doing it so Jeremy could play.

Bischoff screamed. He called for another time-out.

Hank was finished.

Anabel

"Binder, go in."

Anabel could see the words on the coach's lips, even from this far distance.

Jeremy was the only guard left. He was the only kid on the team who could handle the ball. Mr. Bischoff wouldn't have a choice. How lucky. How wonderful. Anabel watched as Hank came in off the court and Jeremy stood up. Something passed between them. They smiled. Jeremy handed Hank something from his pocket.

Keys. They must be the keys to his grandmother's car. Anabel stole a look to see if Mrs. Binder had seen. But she was just clapping wildly like she always did.

Then it all came together. It all made sense, like a perfect handshake.

"Look," Anabel said to Jeremy's grandmother. "He's going in."

Mrs. Binder sat up and strained to look down onto the court.

"Oh, yes. He's going in to play," she said. She started clapping louder.

The boys all looked real tired. Anabel saw her brother and recognized the face. Tired. Nervous, and being so nervous makes you more tired. Michael was bent over, with his thumbs hooked in the armholes of his jersey. His arms dangling, trying to rest. Tyler Bischoff looked miserable. The more his father yelled, the more he put up bad outside shots. Air balls.

Anabel looked down at the court again. Jeremy was playing great. He moved the ball around. You could hear him shouting out directions. He was taking control of the team and it was working.

North Bridge scored on their first possession. The whole place cheered even though Hollis was still ahead by ten points. Another cheer went up from the spectators as North Bridge blocked a shot and got the rebound. Jeremy was bringing the ball back down carefully. He set up his players. Suddenly the crowd around them was stamping their feet and shouting. North Bridge had scored two times in a row. They were only down by six. Anabel reached down for Jeremy's grandmother and took her arm.

"Get up," she said.

Jeremy's grandmother looked up. "Why. Is it over?"

"No," Anabel said. "We're going to win this time."

Nathan

Nathan still hadn't gone in. He made sure to keep his eyes on the game. Maybe his father would notice his great concentration skills. And that would be that.

And then Matt King fouled out. Hank was already out. Jeremy was playing because Hank had set it up to happen that way. The only one who didn't realize this, of course, was the coach. However, what this meant was that Nathan was the only one on the bench who hadn't gone in yet.

And then Tyler Bischoff twists his ankle.

They were down by one point and there were five minutes left on the clock. This is not how Nathan had imagined it. The coach of the other team was certainly not his Uncle Troy. He wasn't black. He was short and bald and very white, pink, in fact. And Nathan's father had certainly showed no signs of recognition when this Hollis coached strutted across the floor to his side of the gym.

"Thomas, go in for Tyler."

He almost didn't hear it. Mr. Bischoff had to say it again. Making Mr. Bischoff say something twice is not a good idea. Hank slapped Nathan on the back.

"Go in," Hank said. "You're in." He gave Nathan a push.

"I can't," Nathan said. He stood up.

"You can," Hank said. "Look, Jeremy's out there. Just watch for the ball. Get open."

"Who am I guarding?"

"That kid, number fifteen." Hank called out. Nathan was almost at the scoring table, checking in.

While he waited to go in, Nathan glanced over to the other bench. Number fifteen was the kid with the mustache. Nathan took one look up into the bleachers just as the timekeeper buzzed him into the game.

"Subs," the referee called out.

Nathan saw his father about midway up. He was smiling and clapping with one hand against his knee. In his other hand he had his digital camera with the ridiculous long lens, poised like someone from *ESPN* magazine. Nathan's mother was holding the baby on her lap and making her hands clap, too. It was like a surreal joke. On him.

After that everything moved in slow motion and it happened all at once.

Nathan's leg immediately felt like rubber. And he tasted a funny taste in his mouth, like metal.

Adrenaline or lactic acid buildup in his muscles.

So fear does have a taste. Nathan made a note of that in his mind as the game resumed play.

Jeremy passed the ball to Nathan. It slammed into his hands hard, but somehow Nathan caught it. All he could see were the kids around him. Moving. Trying to take the ball from him.

Pass it. He had to pass it.

Players were moving all over. Shouting. Calling out.

There. There someone was open. Nathan threw a good hard chest pass. He was relieved. The ball was out of his hands. The kid who caught the ball puts it right up.

Score.

Good. Now move, Nathan thought.

Cut across. Get open.

But suddenly the referee blew the whistle. "Time-out!"

The North Bridge team hurried over to the sideline. Someone from Nathan's side had called the time-out. *What for?*

"Nathan! What are you doing? What the hell was that?" Mr. Bischoff screamed.

"Me?" Nathan asked. *What was the coach talking about?*

"You . . . you passed the ball to the other team.

You just passed the ball. . . ." You could just tell Mr. Bischoff was holding the rest of his sentence inside and it wasn't going to be pretty. He was controlling himself. Barely.

Nathan looked up, trying to remember what had just happened. How could he have done that? What was he going to do now?

Finally Nathan said, "He was the only one open."

GAME

G ame.

  North Bridge @ Hollis. League play-off.

The North Bridge coach has just called for a time-out. Apparently one of their players lost possession by passing the ball to the other team. Hollis scored. North Bridge now has no time-outs remaining. There are three and a half minutes left.

50–47 Hollis.

There now seems to be some general confusion on the court. The North Bridge players appear disheartened by that last turnover. This is understandable, since Nathan Thomas, number three, passed the ball to the other team. Their coach has taken a seat on the bench and is holding his head in his hands. Hollis takes advantage of this moment by stealing the ball from number fifty-four, Harrison Neeley. They make their way down the court. North Bridge seems to have regained some energy under the direction of their point guard, number five, Jeremy Binder. You can hear his voice directing his teammates. His confidence is infectious. All they need are three points to tie up the game. So far North Bridge has been extremely effective in keeping Hollis out of the paint. Hollis is playing a game of catch with each other, unable to get an open shot. Jeremy Binder is running back and forth under the net, forcing the trap and forcing Hollis to pass each time.

The strategy works: Hollis loses the ball on a bounce pass. King throws the ball up court to Binder. Hollis is back on defense in a matter of seconds. They are determined not to give North Bridge this chance to score.

Neeley sets a screen at the three-point line, Binder uses the screen, pumps, fakes, and takes the shot. The ball arches in the air, hits the rim, and bounces in.

It is all tied up. 50–50. Forty-five seconds remaining.

The crowd is on its feet, stomping and shouting.

Hollis has possession. They are wasting the clock hoping to get the last shot off without leaving North Bridge any time to score again. Hollis is passing the ball back and forth at the three-point line. A dangerous crosscourt pass, and suddenly Binder jumps in and steals the ball. Binder throws a baseball pass down the court to Nathan Thomas. There is no one around him. Thomas dribbles the ball twice and turns to the hoop. He has a wide-open shot but he seems to hesitate.

He lifts his arms and then *bam*!

Number fifteen for Hollis blocks the shot. But wait . . . with ten seconds left the whistle shrieks and the referee calls a foul. The coach for Hollis is running up and down the court.

"Two shots?" he is yelling. "Are you kidding? He wasn't shooting. That kid never shoots. He hasn't made one shot all year."

The Hollis coach is thrown out of the game. The North Bridge coach has taken his head out of his hands but is attending to one of his players, apparently his son. The player is holding his ankle and is refusing to return to the game. Nathan Thomas is now standing at the foul line.

Thomas looks down at his feet. He shifts his toes toward the basketball. The referee blows the whistle and hands the ball back to Thomas. This is it. Last chance.

It seems every great game comes down to a moment like this. Thomas lifts his right arm slowly, balancing the ball with his left. He stares hard at the basket as if he is visualizing his shot. He is thinking of something. He smiles. He bends his knees and jumps.

Someone in the bleachers has a camera and has just set the perfect angle and depth of field to capture the shooter, the basket, the court. Even the scoreboard with its yellow glowing numbers can be seen through the viewfinder. The clock stopped at three seconds. But just before the shutter snaps, a toddler in the next seat kicks out his foot in one quick jerking motion, tapping the camera just a tad. What is revealed when the photo comes up on the computer screen is a slightly tilted image of two hands poised in the air in perfect form; just behind them and somehow out of focus is the ball, hitting inside the rim of the basket before it drops into the net.

Hollis has two seconds left, but they never get the ball past the half-court line.

North Bridge wins. 51–50.

Amazing.

Hank

Nathan's parents knew all along. At least, his mother did. Hank heard them talking about it after the game. He figured Nathan was going to have to face them. He wondered what Nathan's dad must be thinking. He must have seen Nathan play. Or not play. And then play. Sort of. Badly.

Nathan's dad must have figured it out.

Maybe not.

Parents don't see the most obvious things half the time. Most of the time. They see what *they* think is important. They see what they want to see. Hank figured his parents probably saw him play the worst game of his life and get pulled out for good. They were probably dying right at this very moment. Planning to sell the house. Or hiring a professional at-home basketball coach. Or investing in some lacrosse equipment.

Hank could see Nathan's parents standing together by the door, waiting for Nathan to come out of the locker room. He could just barely hear what they were saying. His dad looked confused. His mom didn't.

"He was having fun," Nathan's mom was saying.

"That didn't look like much fun," his dad answered.

"He made the winning shot."

"What game were *you* watching. Yeah, he made his second foul shot. It was a miracle. He's terrible, Denise. He's really terrible."

"Yeah, he's pretty terrible," his mother said quietly.

And then all of a sudden, they started laughing. Hank could hear them. They seemed to share a secret between them that made everything funnier than it was. Even their little baby starting giggling. They moved on toward the exit. Hank stopped walking.

"What's going on?" Nathan came up beside Hank.

"Your parents," Hank said.

"Yeah, they must know about me now," Nathan said.

The crowd for the next game were starting to pour into the gym. More parents climbing up the bleachers checking out the situation, looking for the right place to sit. A whole new set of kids took their seats on the bench. They looked like fifth graders, maybe. Ten and eleven year olds. Their coach was talking to them.

"This is it," the coach was saying. He was kneeling on the floor in front of the bench with his clipboard resting on his knee.

"You're not worried about telling them the truth anymore?" Hank asked Nathan as they started walking, making their way past the bleachers.

"Na," Nathan said. "They don't look too upset, do they? I think they knew all along anyway."

"You do?"

"Yeah."

The fifth-grade coach was still talking to his young team. "I don't want any stupid mistakes out there. Connor! Are you paying attention? Listen up. This isn't fun and games. . . ."

Hank and Nathan looked at each other.

"What about you?" Nathan asked his friend. "What about *your* dad?"

Hank looked around. His parents weren't in the gym. They must be waiting for him out in the hall or in the parking lot, even.

"What?" Hank asked, although he knew exactly what Nathan meant. It had been Hank's chance. It would have been one of those games his dad was always talking about. It might have been one of those games for Hank, five seconds on the clock, fans on their feet, tied score. . . .

Just like his dad always said when he was watching that one guy, that one moment, on TV.

"Will your dad be mad at you?" Nathan interrupted his thoughts.

"He'll get over it," Hank said.

"You sure?"

"Yeah."

Hank and Nathan caught up to Nathan's parents. Hank watched Nathan's dad put his arm around his son. They said hello to Hank, shook his hand, and then turned into the hall. Hank followed behind.

"Good game, son," Nathan's dad said. He was tall, Hank noticed.

"Dad?" Nathan started.

"You sure came through in the clutch," his dad went on.

"Dad?"

"Yes? You have something to tell me?"

Nathan couldn't see it, but Hank did. Right then, Nathan's mother jabbed her elbow into her husband's ribs. He sounded with a puff of air.

"Dad, I—" Nathan began again.

"You were wonderful, Nat," his mother interrupted. "I'm so glad we came."

"So am I," his dad said. You could tell he really meant that.

When they headed out to their car, Hank could see they were all smiling and it made him smile, too.

Until he saw his parents' car.

The engine was running. They were already inside. Not a good sign.

Hank

Hank knew his dad and mom weren't going to be "mad" at him. They never got mad. It would be worse than that. They'd be disappointed.

As Hank walked toward his car, he thought about that.

Disappointment.

He coulda been a hero.

But then sometimes there is a moment when you decide there *has* to be, in fact, there *is* something more important than winning. More important than even *playing*. Hank opened the car door and slid into the backseat knowing he was right. *Knowing* he had done the right thing.

It was just starting to rain. It was one of those surprising, all of a sudden really heavy rains, with big loud drops pelting the windshield.

"Just in time," his mother said.

His father flipped on the wipers. At least the sound would drown out his parents' disappointment in him for the ride home, anyway.

But his dad didn't shift the car into drive. Instead he turned around and leaned his arm on the back of the seat. "You did a really great thing out there for your friend," he said.

Hank noticed his mother had tears in her eyes, but that didn't mean anything; she cried all the time. She cried at phone company commercials. She cried when she walked in on the last minute and a half of a corny TV movie.

"You're a very special boy," his mother said.

"We couldn't be more proud of you, Hank," his dad told him.

And Hank knew he was a hero.

Jeremy

They never talked about it. Jeremy never said, *"Hey, Hank, that was a really incredible thing you did for me out there. Sacrificing yourself so I could play."*

And then Hank would shrug and say, *"That's what friends do for each other."*

No, it never happened like that.

They never even mentioned it.

Jeremy looked up at his grandmother as she made her way down from the bleachers after the game. She was using the tops of other people's heads to balance herself and apologizing the whole way. It was kind of funny. Jeremy smiled as he jingled the keys to his grandmother's car in his pocket. He'd have to

remember to put them back in the little box in the
tall wooden thingy with hooks, where he was supposed to hang his sweatshirt, when he got home.

The keys would always be there, which was good
to know even though he didn't feel like he needed
them.

Jeremy was tired and sweaty. But he felt good. His
grandmother was reaching the bottom step. Jeremy
reached out and took her hand so she could step
down onto the gym floor.

"What a good game, Jeremy. How exciting." She
was practically out of breath. "Do you want to stop
and get some ice cream," she asked.

"No, thanks," he answered, and she didn't press
him.

Actually Jeremy was looking forward to getting
home. He knew there was leftover homemade maca-
roni and cheese.

His favorite.

HIGH
SCHOOL

NORTH BRIDGE IN SEMIFINALS

(con't. from page B1)

"MOST OF US GIRLS PLAYED ON the middle-school travel teams," Anabel Morrisey said on the bus ride up to Colby High. "We've been working hard toward this night, some of us since sixth or seventh grade."

The big game was only a couple of hours away, but senior captain Morrisey seemed calm and collected. When asked what she thought about the scouts from UNC and UConn who would be at the game to watch her, she shrugged.

"It's just a game," she answered. "I mean, it's fun and it's real exciting sometimes. I love being part of a team. But I learned a long time ago where basketball, or any sport for that matter, should fit into your life."

As the bus got closer to Colby High, the girls got quieter. There was a tension building, an anticipation. No one knew what the outcome of the game would be, but it was clear these girls deserved to make it this far. It was obvious that Anabel Morrisey had won, even before the first whistle was blown.

OVERTIME

Anabel Morrisey is senior captain of the North
Bridge girls' basketball team. Her coach, Pat
Trimboli, calls her a "pure shooter." Scouts from several Division I women's teams have come to watch
her play. Yesterday she got a call from an assistant
coach at the University of Connecticut. They want to
meet and talk with her. It's all pretty exciting.

Still, everyone says the most impressive thing
about Anabel is her perspective on the whole thing.
Her brother, Michael, is her personal trainer and her
biggest fan. Her dad comes to every game, and her
mom comes to as many as she can.

Jeremy's father *did* come back for real. It was one day somewhere between the end of middle school and the beginning of high school. Jeremy was playing in an AAU tournament upstate. Jeremy's dad was standing in the back of the gym watching, just the way Jeremy had always imagined. And he *was* proud and amazed to see his son play, but by that time Jeremy had stopped looking for him. Jeremy never even saw him standing there.

He left before the end of the game, and only Jeremy's grandmother saw him. She didn't stop her son from leaving, and she never told Jeremy she had seen him. She thought, one day when he was old enough, maybe Jeremy would go and find his father. Maybe he wouldn't.

Jeremy earned his varsity letter as a freshman in both basketball and track. He's thinking of applying to Brown. They've seen his films. He's interested in premed.

Hank played basketball on the high-school team for two seasons, but somewhere along the line he found that music was his passion. He had a garage band that practiced, of course, in his garage. His dad had the whole inside lined with special foam that made their recording sound better. And he had an electrician install an extra circuit box to accommodate the equipment. And just this month, Hank's band has gotten two gigs in NYC.

The name of his band is Tuna Fish Railroad, for no reason at all.

Nathan didn't play basketball anymore, except sometimes in gym class or outside in the summer. He played one more year in middle school, on the seventh-grade travel team, and then in eighth grade he didn't make the team, which ended up being the best thing that could have happened. Nathan joined the debate team in eighth grade. He did so well that his guidance counselor suggested he join Future Business Leaders of America when he got to high school. Which he did. One thing lead to another, and a speech Nathan perfected in his public speaking class won him honorable mention at the FBLA regional competition. His speech was about teamwork. This year Nathan won first place in the public speaking category, and he is supposed to fly to Austin, Texas, for the national competition.

Nathan, Jeremy, and Hank went to every one of Anabel's games that they could. Anabel and Nathan went to every one of Hank and Jeremy's games. If they were watching, they sucked on oversized lollipops sold in the concession stand and screamed wildly for Jeremy and Hank or Anabel and all the other players on the North Bridge High school basketball teams.

But wherever they were, whatever was going on, they could always bring back that sixth-grade year with one little phrase.

"He was the only one open."

And they would all crack up laughing. That was the year they began to realize what was important. And what was not.

So if Anabel was ever feeling down or "not good enough"; when Nathan needed to lighten up; when Hank was feeling too pressured; when Jeremy was feeling like he *still* didn't belong, they'd shake hands with each other.

A bang, a wiggle, a thumb-touching thing, and a firm grip ending.

A promise.

And it was still theirs.